'Dario, are you even listening to me?'

He forced his gaze back to Megan's face. Her pale skin had acquired a healthy sun-burnished glow in the last week, her cheeks now a bright scarlet hue even more tempting than that damn bikini. He wanted to lick that fluttering pulse in her collarbone so much that he could almost taste her sweet, spicy aroma on his tongue.

The way he had every night in his dreams.

Her eyes had widened. Was that trepidation or shock he could see in them, their misty green bright with stunned knowledge? Then she rolled her lip under small white teeth and everything inside him shattered. All the smart, practical, moral reasons why he couldn't taste her seemed to explode in a cloud of nuclear fallout.

'Stop biting your lip,' he said, his voice a low, husky croak he barely recognised as his own.

'Dario! Don't speak to me like that.'

He wrapped his hands around her upper arms and hauled her to him.

Then all coherent thought fled as his lips landed on succulent skin and his hands captured the lush curves that had finally pushed him over the edge into madness.

One Night With Consequences

When one night…leads to pregnancy!

When succumbing to a night of unbridled desire
it's impossible to think past the morning after!

But, with the sheets barely settled,
that little blue line appears on the pregnancy test and it
doesn't take long to realise that one night of white-hot
passion has turned into a lifetime of consequences!

Only one question remains:

How do you tell a man you've just met
that you're about to share more than just his bed?

Find out in:

Look for more **One Night With Consequences** stories
coming soon!

THE VIRGIN'S SHOCK BABY

BY
HEIDI RICE

First Published in Great Britain 2017
By Mills & Boon, an imprint of HarperCollins*Publishers*
1 London Bridge Street, London, SE1 9GF

© 2017 Heidi Rice

ISBN: 978-0-263-06990-7

Printed and bound in Great Britain
by CPI Antony Rowe, Chippenham, Wiltshire

USA TODAY bestselling author **Heidi Rice** lives in London, England. She is married with two teenage sons—which gives her rather too much of an insight into the male psyche—and also works as a film journalist. She adores her job, which involves getting swept up in a world of high emotions, sensual excitement, funny, feisty women, sexy, tortured men and glamorous locations where laundry doesn't exist. Once she turns off her computer she often does chores—usually involving laundry!

Books by Heidi Rice

Mills & Boon Modern Romance

Vows They Can't Escape
One Night, So Pregnant!
Too Close for Comfort

Mills & Boon Modern Tempted

Beach Bar Baby
Maid of Dishonour
Cupcakes and Killer Heels
The Good, the Bad and the Wild
On the First Night of Christmas...

Visit the Author Profile page
at millsandboon.co.uk for more titles.

To Bryony, who made sure I gave this story
the depth it deserved.

And Daisy, who talked me off the ledge a few times
while I was doing that!

Dario, Megan and I thank you both sincerely.

PROLOGUE

'DARIO DE ROSSI IS escorting you to the Westchester Ball tomorrow night and you need to seduce him while you're there.'

'What? Why?' Megan Whittaker was fairly sure she'd just been transported into an alternate universe. An alternate universe that was two hundred years past its sell-by date. Either that or her father had lost his mind. Whichever way you looked at it, the demand he had just levelled at her from across his walnut desk in the Manhattan offices of Whittaker Enterprises, without even the hint of a smile on his face, was not good news, because he did not appear to be joking.

'To save Whittaker's from possible annihilation,' her father snapped. 'Don't give me your whipped puppy look, Megan,' he added. 'Do you think I would ask this of you if there were another option?'

'Well, I...' She wanted to believe him, even though she knew his love for Whittaker's had always taken precedence over his love for his daughters.

But unlike her sister, Katie, Megan understood that. Having spent the last four years working her way up to head her own tiny department at Whittaker's, she didn't begrudge him his dedication to the company that had been in their family for five generations.

She also didn't really begrudge him a request so out-side the norm for a father to a daughter, or indeed a boss to his employee. She knew that to be successful in business your personal life had to suffer, and personal loyalties could be tested. But this was… Well… It wasn't even rational. What possible reason could there be for her to seduce any man? Let alone a man like De Rossi, a corporate wolf who had risen through the ranks of New York business society in the last ten years to become one of its prime movers and shakers.

Quite apart from anything else, if her father was looking for a femme fatale, surely he must know Megan was not the best candidate for the job.

She simply did not have the necessary temperament, equipment or experience. She had always been more comfortable in business suits and flats than cocktail dresses and heels. She found going to the beauty salon tedious, the concentration on her appearance a waste of time and money. Her intellect and her work ethic were so much more important. And after the few fumbled encounters she'd had at college, she'd been beyond grateful to discover she comprehensively lacked her mother's voracious and indiscriminate libido. At twenty-four, she was still technically speaking a virgin, for goodness' sake! These days she would much rather spend her small amount of free time watching TV boxsets with a nice glass of Pouilly Fuissé, than finding a man—especially as the judicious use of a vibrator could take care of her needs without all the awkwardness and disappointment.

'Someone's buying up all our stock,' her father said, the vein pulsing at his temple starting to disturb Megan. 'I'm almost certain it's him. And if it is him, we're in serious trouble. We're exposed. We have to stay his hand. That means making sacrifices for the good of the company.'

'But I don't understand how...'

'You don't have to understand. What you have to do is get an invitation back to his penthouse so we can discover if it is him. If you can find out which of our shareholders he's targeting that would be even better. Then we might have some hope of keeping the bastard off our back until I can secure new capital investment.'

'You expect me to seduce him for the purposes of industrial espionage?' Megan tried to clarify where her father was going with this, as something became devastatingly obvious to her. He had to be exceptionally stressed to believe she could pull such a plan off with her limited skills, which meant the company must be in serious financial difficulties.

'You have your mother's face and figure, Megan. And you're not a lesbian... Are you?'

Her face coloured, the heat racing up her neck, the impatient enquiry mortifying her. 'What? Of course not, but...'

'Then what's the damn problem? Surely there must be enough of that oversexed bitch in you somewhere to know how to seduce this bastard. It's built into your DNA, all you have to do is locate it.' Her father was becoming increasingly frantic. The bitterness in his voice at the mention of her mother made Megan's stomach knot.

Her father never mentioned her mother. Not ever. Alexis Whittaker had abandoned all three of them—her father, herself and her little sister, Katie—not long after Katie's birth, and had died ten years ago when her Italian boyfriend's Ferrari had plummeted from a clifftop road on the island of Capri. Megan could still remember her father coming to tell her the news at her boarding school in Cornwall, his face white with an agonising combination of grief, pain and humiliation. And she could remember the same hollow sensation in her stomach.

Her mother had been a social butterfly, stunningly beautiful, flamboyant and reckless—with everyone's life including her own. Megan could barely remember her; she'd never come to visit her daughters, which was why their father had shipped them off to board at St Grey's as soon as they were old enough.

The hollow confusion had turned to panic though, when paparazzi photos of her and Katie at the funeral had appeared on the Internet. They had been forced to leave the only real home they had ever known, chased out by the photographers wanting to get a glimpse of the 'grief-stricken' Whittaker sisters, and the salacious whispers about their mother's infidelities, spread by some of the other girls at St Grey's. Her father had moved them to an apartment ten blocks from his own on Fifth Avenue in New York, employed a housekeeper and a security guard, enrolled them in an exclusive private school and made the effort to visit them at least once a month. And eventually the media storm surrounding Alexis Whittaker's wicked ways and her untimely death had died down.

But ever since Megan had been ripped away from St Grey's, she had promised herself two things: she would protect the sister she loved from the fallout of her mother's disgrace, and she would work herself to the bone to prove to her father that she was nothing like the woman who had given birth to them.

And up until this moment, she had thought she'd succeeded. With her second objective at least. Katie, unfortunately, appeared to be almost as wild as their mother, despite Megan's best efforts to tame her rebellious temperament.

Megan, though, had concentrated on making her father proud. She'd got a first at Cambridge two years ahead of her peers in computer science. And then an MBA at

Harvard Business School specialising in e-commerce. To prove herself worthy, not just to her father but to her colleagues at Whittaker's, she'd refused his offer of a vanity position and had instead started on the ground floor of the building in Midtown. After six months in the mailroom, she'd applied for an internship in the tech department. It had taken her three years to work her way up the ladder from there, rung by torturous rung. Her recent promotion had put her in charge of the company's small three-person e-commerce department, finally proving once and for all that her mother's shameful behaviour had no bearing on who she was. Until this moment.

How could her father even consider asking her to seduce De Rossi? Did he expect her to have sex with the man, too?

'I can't do it,' she said.

'Why the hell not?'

Because I'm about as far from being De Rossi's ideal woman as Daffy Duck is from Jessica Rabbit.

'Because it wouldn't be ethical,' she managed, recoiling from the hot flash of memory from the only time she'd ever met De Rossi in the flesh.

He'd certainly made an impression.

She'd heard of him, but the gossip hadn't prepared her for the staggeringly handsome man who had arrived at the Met Ball with supermodel Giselle Monroe hanging off his arm like the latest fashion accessory. The brute force of his powerful body had barely been contained by the expertly tailored designer suit, and his bold heated gaze had raked over her when they'd been introduced by her father. The knowledge in his ice-blue eyes had disturbed her on a purely visceral level. And set off a thousand tiny explosions of sensation over every inch of exposed skin.

She'd been careful to avoid De Rossi for the rest of the evening, because she'd known instinctively the man was not just tall, dark and handsome, but also extremely dangerous—to her peace of mind.

'Don't be naïve.' Her father flicked a chilling glare at her. 'There are no ethics in business. Not when it comes to the bottom line. De Rossi certainly doesn't have any, so we can't afford to have any either.'

'But how did you even persuade him to take me to the ball?' Megan said, becoming desperate herself.

'It's a charity ball. He's paying for a table. You're going to be Whittaker's representative there. I asked him to escort you as a courtesy to me; he's a member of my club.'

So she had officially become a pity date—which would have been mortifying, if her father's ulterior motive wasn't a thousand times worse.

'De Rossi's only weakness that I could find is for beautiful women,' her father continued in the same deceptively pragmatic tone. As if he were talking sense, instead of insanity. 'Not that it's exactly a weakness. He's never been foolish enough to marry one of them, unlike me. And he never keeps them longer than a few months. But he's between women at the moment, according to Annalise, who keeps up with this nonsense,' he said, mentioning his mistress. 'And he never has one out of his bed for long. Which gives you all the opportunity you need. He'll be on the hunt and I'm putting you in his path. All you need to do is get his attention.' The dispassionate statement had shame burning the back of Megan's neck. 'Get an invite to his penthouse on Central Park West,' her father continued. 'Once he takes you there, you can get access to his computer and his files. Computers are your forte, are they not?'

That he'd thought this scenario through in such detail wasn't helping the chill spreading through Megan's abdomen—or the flush of awareness flaming across her scalp.

'But anything he has on there will be password protected,' she said, trying to be practical.

'I have his passwords.'

'How?'

'It's not important. The important thing is to get access to his computer before he changes them. Which means acting quickly and concisely.'

And setting her up as some kind of Mata Hari? The idea would almost be funny if it weren't so appalling.

'You can't ask me to do this,' said Megan. She'd always strived so hard to please her father, to prove herself worthy of his trust. There weren't many things she wouldn't do for him, but this request scared her on so many levels. 'You wouldn't ask me to, if I were your son,' she added, trying to appeal to her father's sense of justice. He wasn't a bad man, he was fair and, in his own gruff, distant way, he loved her and Katie. Obviously he was so stressed he had completely lost his grip on reality. But he had to be under a huge amount of pressure, if De Rossi was sniffing about the company.

She knew enough about De Rossi's business practices from the financial press to know that once his conglomerate got their hooks into your stock you were as good as dead in the water. He was famous for asset stripping. If he really was planning a hostile takeover, he could reduce Whittaker's to rubble in weeks, a legacy company destroyed in a heartbeat simply to feed his insatiable appetite for wealth at any cost. But her father's solution was beyond desperate, not to mention illegal, and doomed to failure. She had to make him see that, and find another way.

'If I had a son and De Rossi was gay, that would be an option.' Instead of looking persuaded, the tic in her father's cheek went ballistic. 'As neither is the case, it's a moot point.'

The blush seared her skin, the knot in her stomach tightening into a hollow ball of anxiety. It was no good, she was going to be forced to state the obvious.

'De Rossi might as well be gay for all the interest he's likely to take in me. He dates supermodels.'

And I'm hardly supermodel material.

At five-foot-five, and with the lush curves she had inherited from her mother, Megan had felt like an overendowed pixie next to the slim, stunning woman who had fawned over De Rossi at the Met Ball.

But Megan's lack of appeal to men had always felt like a boon. She didn't want to become any man's decorative accessory. Especially not a man like De Rossi, who even on their brief acquaintance she suspected was as ruthless with women as he was in his business dealings.

She could control those mini explosions. They were nothing more than a biological reaction.

'Don't sell yourself short.' Her father huffed, looking exasperated now as well as desperate. 'You have enough of your mother's charms to attract him if you put your mind to it.'

'But I—'

'If you don't do it, there's only one other person I can ask.'

Megan's panic downgraded. Thank goodness, he had someone else he could ask. She would not have to even attempt something that was bound to humiliate and degrade her, and was extremely unlikely to be successful. 'Who?'

'Your sister, Katie.'

The panic went from ten to ninety in a nanosecond.

'But Katie's only nineteen,' she cried, shocked. 'And she's in art school.'

After an endless string of school expulsions and acting out against their father's authority, Katie had finally found her passion as a talented and brilliant artist. And she didn't give a fig about Whittaker's.

'An art school I pay for,' her father remarked, the dispassionate expression chilling Megan to the bone. Katie and her father had been at loggerheads for years—ever since the sisters had moved to New York after their mother's death. It had taken Megan months to persuade their father to pay for the exclusive academy that had only offered Katie a partial scholarship—something she had never told her sister. She didn't know how Katie would react if she discovered their father was paying some of her tuition fees and was prepared to pull the plug on the dreams she'd worked so hard for to save Whittaker's. But Megan doubted it would be good.

'Your sister is also as reckless and wild as your mother,' her father added. 'Given the right incentive, I think we both know she'd pass this assignment with flying colours.'

No, she wouldn't, she'd be crushed, Megan thought.

Katie was as lively and spirited as Megan was cautious and grounded. But for all her recklessness, she also had an open and easily bruised heart—and absolutely no regard for business ethics or expediency. Katie would be appalled that their father could ask such a thing of either one of them. And Katie's own worst enemy was usually Katie. She was volatile and unpredictable, especially if she was hurt. So much so that Megan had no idea what she'd do if forced into this situation by their father. She could have a mad passionate affair with De Rossi or annoy him so much he'd destroy Whittaker's just for the hell of it. But one thing was for sure, putting a hothead like Katie into the path of someone as ruthless as De Rossi would be a car crash of epic proportions, and Katie would be the one who got destroyed.

'The only reason I haven't already asked her is because

she knows nothing about computers,' her father said. 'And De Rossi likes his lovers more mature, according to Annalise,' he added. 'You've got a better chance. But if you leave me with no choice I will have to explain to your sister that if she wants to stay at her fancy art school she will have to—'

'Okay, I'll do it,' Megan jumped in, before her father could state the unthinkable. 'I'll give it my best shot.'

Even if her best shot had very little chance of being a success, her pride and her ethics felt like a small price to pay to save her sister from heartbreak—and Whittaker's from guaranteed annihilation.

'Good girl, Megan,' her father said. 'Take the day off tomorrow. Annalise will accompany you to select an outfit suitable for the occasion and take you to her beautician to get you properly prepared.'

'Okay,' she said, feeling dazed at the enormity of what she had just agreed to—and how ill-prepared she was for the challenge. Annalise's alluring sense of style and supreme sexual confidence had always intimidated Megan.

'Don't disappoint me. Whittaker's is counting on you,' her father finished, dismissing her as he turned back to the papers on his desk.

'I know and I won't,' she murmured, trying to sound confident.

But as she returned to her small office on the building's tenth floor, the pressure of what she had to achieve sat in her belly like a brick. An annoyingly hot brick seeping an uncontrollable and completely unregulated warmth throughout her body.

She didn't feel confident; she felt like a sacrifice, about to be staked out in the wolf's lair, with nothing to protect her but a designer gown and heels and an overpriced beautician's appointment.

CHAPTER ONE

'No way, Katie. You need to stay in your room when he gets here.' Megan's hand trembled as she picked up one of the diamond drop earrings Annalise had loaned her to match the sleek, blue, satin, floor-length gown it had taken her father's mistress an eternity to select during their endless shopping expedition that afternoon. The sting as the thin silver spike penetrated the rarely used hole in her lobe did nothing to calm the rapid flutter of Megan's heartbeat. She breathed deeply and picked up the other earring. She needed to stop hyperventilating or she was liable to pass out before De Rossi even arrived.

'But I want to meet him, to make sure he doesn't take advantage of you,' Katie said, the fire in her eyes accompanied by a petulant pout. 'He's rich, arrogant and scarily gorgeous. You've got zero experience of guys like him. Did you see the cover shot of him on that boring business magazine you get? He even looks hot in one of those stuffy suits.'

Yes, she had seen the magazine, she'd even re-read the interview with De Rossi to give herself some useful topics of conversation. But all the article had really done—illustrated with all those photos of him looking broad and muscular and indomitable—was make her panic increase. And Katie's misguided attempts to protect her were not helping.

'What if he tries to ravish you?' Katie added, the battle she'd been waging for the last two hours—to stand between Megan and De Rossi's super-human seduction skills—starting to wear on Megan's already frazzled nerves.

De Rossi was due to arrive in less than five minutes and Katie's misguided reading of the situation was the last thing Megan needed. But she would never tell Katie the truth. That the only thing standing between them and financial ruin was Megan's mission to seduce De Rossi—not the other way around—because that would only make Katie worry more about Megan's date in the lion's den. And Megan was already panicking enough for both of them.

She'd spent most of her life shielding her sister, ever since the day she'd stood beside a nine-year-old Katie at their mother's graveside and held her as her little sister shed real tears for a woman who had abandoned them.

She was not about to stop now.

But sometimes shielding Katie from the realities of life could be very trying. Megan poked the second earring into her earlobe with an unsteady hand and absorbed the sting, attempting to tune out Katie's next offensive.

'I can't believe you won't even let me meet him. All I want to do is make sure he knows not to mess with you.' Katie stood defiantly behind her, every sinew in her slim, coltish body fraught with challenge and righteous determination. 'At least promise me you won't let him lure you back to his love nest on Central Park West.'

'His *what* nest?' Megan would have laughed at the term, if her heart hadn't just jumped into her throat.

'Don't look like that.' Katie rolled her eyes, frustrated. 'That's what they called it in Giselle Monroe's piece in the *Post*. Didn't you read it?'

'No, I did not, and you shouldn't have either. It's salacious gossip.' The last thing she needed to read was the model's kiss-and-tell account of De Rossi's sexual prowess when she was nervous enough already.

'According to Giselle,' Katie continued undeterred, 'the guy's insatiable in the sack. He can make a woman—'

'Katie, for goodness' sake, shut up!' She swung round on the stool. 'I didn't read it, because I didn't need to. This isn't a proper date.' Even if the memory of one look from the man was still giving her goosebumps a month after the fact. 'Dad asked him to escort me. He may not even turn up.' The hope that he might have forgotten the arrangement had guilt coalescing in her stomach to go with the panic.

She was Whittaker's only hope. She'd promised to do this thing, even if the computer codes buried in her purse were burning a hole in her conscience.

The sound of the front door buzzer made them both jump.

'So he's not gonna show, huh?' Katie said, looking triumphant.

Megan cursed under her breath, and stood to check out her reflection. The gown was sleek and simple in its elegance, the bias-cut satin snug enough to enhance her curves without offering them up on a platter. Or at least, that was what Annalise had insisted.

Diamonds sparkled in the thin straps that held up the bodice, which plunged low enough to entice but not low enough to give Megan an anxiety attack. Yet. A faux-fur wrap to hold off the night-time chill in late April, and four-inch heels—which were as high as she could go without risking a twisted ankle—an elaborate up-do that held her unruly hair in some kind of order, a five-hundred-dollar make-up session and the delicate diamond drop earrings completed the outfit. Annalise had told her the ensemble screamed sophistication and purpose, rather than panic and desperation.

Megan wasn't so sure.

She heard the front door of the apartment being opened by their housekeeper, Lydia Brady, and the low murmur of a deep masculine voice.

Awareness rippled up her spine and she grasped her sister's wrists. 'Stay here, Katie, I'm warning you. This is going to be humiliating enough without you there making me feel even more self-conscious.'

Katie pulled her hands free, the spark of defiance disappearing for the first time in hours. 'Why would it be humiliating?'

'Because I'm not his type and he's only taking me as a favour to Dad.'

And Dad expects me to seduce him. Somehow. And then commit a crime to save Whittaker's.

'What do you mean, you're not his type?' Katie's gaze travelled over Megan's outfit, the appreciation in her wide green eyes making Megan's heart pound even harder. 'You look absolutely stunning. Just like Mum. I wish I had at least a few of your curves.' She flung her arms around Megan's shoulders, holding her tight for a few precious seconds. 'You're going to knock his designer socks off, you silly moo,' Katie whispered in her ear, before she drew back. Warmth suffused Megan.

Even when she was being a pain in the backside, Katie was Megan's greatest cheerleader and her best friend.

'Which is precisely why you need me there to make sure he doesn't get any ideas,' Katie added, in case Megan hadn't figured that out already after the four-hour campaign. 'Are you absolutely sure you don't want me to threaten him with my kick-boxing skills?'

'You gave up kick-boxing after two sessions,' Megan pointed out.

'What if I threaten to macramé him to death instead, then?' Katie offered—probably only half joking. 'I did a killer macramé piece for my course.'

The chuckle that popped out of Megan's mouth was part gratitude and part hysteria. Whatever happened with De Rossi, her life was likely to be irrevocably changed once tonight was over. Because she'd either be in his bed, or in a prison cell. Her sister's silly joke helped to ground her, though, and confirm what she already knew: that protecting Katie and her dreams, and protecting Whittaker's, were worth sacrificing her self-respect and throwing herself at De Rossi tonight.

All Megan had to do was figure out how to do that without having a nervous breakdown.

Lydia Brady stepped into the room. 'Mr De Rossi has arrived, Megan.' The older woman smiled. 'You look beautiful, dear.'

'Thank you, Lydia.' Nerves screamed across her bare shoulders, and the hot brick in her stomach sank lower.

Letting go of her sister's hands, she walked towards the dressing-room door, affecting the expression she had practised in the mirror for hours last night. Polite, confident and, she hoped, at least a little alluring.

Her heels echoed on the marble flooring as she made her way down the corridor, but as she turned into the apartment's plush lobby area all the air seized in her lungs and her steps faltered.

Dario De Rossi looked up from adjusting his cuffs, his crystal-blue eyes locking on her face like a tractor beam, and sending a sizzle of electric energy through her body.

The man looked devastating in a tux. Tall and broad, his powerful body only made more intimidating by the classic black tailoring, which emphasised the magnificent width of his shoulders, the leanness of his waist and the length of his legs.

How tall was he? At least three inches above her father's six feet.

She took a careful breath and forced herself to carry on walking, grateful her wrap covered her cleavage when the assessing gaze roamed down, setting off a series of mini explosions and making her insides grow hot.

'*Buonasera*, Megan.'

His English was so perfect, with only the slightest hint of his Italian heritage, it felt strangely intimate to have him greet her in his native language. The way the deep husky rumble of his voice skated across already oversensitive flesh, though, was not as disturbing as the dark flash of hunger in his eyes as she drew level.

'*Buonasera,*' she said, answering him in Italian automatically.

He lifted her fingers to his mouth, startling her, and pressed his lips to the knuckles.

The gesture should have been polite, gallant even, but for the way his thumb slid across her palm as he lowered her hand, sending arrows of sensation darting up her arm, and into her torso.

She tugged her hand out of his grasp, shocked by her response, as his gaze roamed up to her hair.

'The colour is natural?' he asked.

'Yes,' she replied, disconcerted by the approval shining in his eyes.

His firm lips lifted in a smile that managed to be both amused and predatory, as if he were a panther, toying with his prey.

'I hope I did not offend you,' he said, the intimacy of his gaze contradicting his apology. The bright blue gaze then dipped to her toes and back, sending seismic ripples over her skin and igniting every pulse point like a firework.

'Relax, *cara mia*.' The rough chuckle scraped across her nerve-endings.

A fiery blush crept up her neck. Was he mocking her?

She looked down at her hands, and forced her fingers to release their death grip on the diamond-encrusted purse. Annalise had told her that looking like a lamb being led to slaughter would not entice any man.

Breathe. Remember to breathe. Breathing is good.

But when she raised her head, he was doing that laser-beam thing again, as if he could see right through her—to the soon-to-be felon beneath.

'I'm sorry, I'm tired,' she mumbled. 'I've had a very busy day.'

Could she actually sound any *more* inane? Where was all the scintillating conversation about his business acquisitions that she had been working on for hours?

'Doing what?' he asked.

'Shopping for this dress, mostly. And getting my hair and nails and stuff done,' she replied honestly. Until today she'd had no idea that trawling the designer boutiques of the Upper East Side and spending four hours getting waxed and plucked and pampered to within an inch of her life was more exhausting than hiking up Kilimanjaro.

'Have you, now?' he said, the wry tone making her realise the statement made her sound like a spoilt debutante fishing for a compliment.

Humiliation washed over her.

She knew from the articles she'd devoured about him in the last twenty-four hours that he had been born into one of Rome's most notorious slums. He had to know what true exhaustion was. Everything else about his origins was sketchy, something he refused to talk to the press about, but that simple nugget of information had only intimidated her more. She could well imagine how hard De Rossi must have fought to escape his origins—and how hard he would fight now to keep hold of what he had. And what he wanted to acquire.

Her skin burned, her nipples tightening as his gaze met hers. The cool blue was not as icy as she remembered it from their first brief meeting. His lips quirked.

'It was time and money well spent,' he said, the casual compliment making the flush flare across her collarbone.

Then, to her astonishment, he lifted a hand and tucked his forefinger under her chin. The soft brush of the knuckle was like a zap of electricity, firing down to her core as he lifted her face.

She stiffened, stunned by the enormity of her response to a simple touch. She struggled not to jerk her head away, to submit to the proprietorial caress, despite being brutally aware of the heat now blazing on her cheeks.

What was going on here? Because the amused quirk on his lips had disappeared. Why was he looking at her so intently?

He drew his thumb across her bottom lip.

'You are very beautiful in your own unique way,' he said, his gaze lifting to her chignon. 'Especially that hair.'

He sounded sincere. Why did that make tonight seem all the more terrifying?

She forced a smile, trying desperately to pretend she wasn't burning up inside. But she couldn't resist the involuntary flick of her tongue to moisten lips dried to parchment. He focused on her mouth, and a soft indrawn breath escaped her at the hunger in his eyes.

'The colour reminds me of a naked flame,' he said. 'I wonder if you're as fiery in bed?'

The heat swelling in her abdomen settled uncomfortably between her legs at the boldly sexual comment. She ought to say something provocative back.

But she didn't feel provocative, she felt stunned. And hopelessly aroused. And completely out of her depth. Already.

Dario De Rossi wanted her. And while that should have been very good news, because she was supposed to be seducing him, the power dynamic did not feel as if it was in her favour. Surely her thighs wouldn't be trembling under that hard, heated gaze if it were? She searched her mind for something to say that wouldn't clue him in to how inexperienced she was.

Annalise had told her in no uncertain terms that De Rossi would not find her gaucheness appealing.

Think, Megan, think. What would Mata Hari do?

'That's for me to know,' she finally managed, allowing the desire her body couldn't seem to control to show in her voice. 'And for you to find out, if you dare.'

'There's not much I wouldn't dare, *cara*,' he said, the cynical edge in his tone disturbingly compelling.

His hand dropped, and she couldn't prevent the tiny sob as her body softened in relief.

She was playing a very dangerous game. But she had no choice. She had to brazen this out, pretend she was much more knowing and experienced than she actually was.

Sweeping his hand out in front of him, he smiled, and she became a little fixated on those firm sensual lips.

'Let's get you to the ball, Cinderella.'

She pushed out a strained laugh and walked past him, only to tense as his hand settled on the base of her spine. Sensation flashed down to her bottom, but she carried on walking, acting as if the feel of his hand wasn't burning through her clothing.

The ride down in the lift was excruciating, the deceptively light touch driving her insane. He kept his palm there the whole time, guiding her where he wanted her to go, and not letting her stray more than an inch from his side with the subtlest of gestures. But even so, the heat grew.

As they walked out of the apartment building, past the doorman, her nerves were screaming, the controlling pressure so light it was torture not to stretch against his hold. Her body waged a battle between wanting to kick off her heels and race away from him down the street, while another, much more elemental urge had her longing to ease closer to him and let the heat of his body overwhelm her.

The night chill caught her hair, making the tendrils the stylist had spent an hour carefully teasing out of the chignon dance against her neck. She shivered, the skin there already oversensitised by the feel of his gaze boring into her from behind.

The sleek black limousine was parked at the kerb, a man in a dark suit and a cap waiting for them. The chauffeur opened the door and tipped his hat, giving her a polite smile.

She eased into the shadowed interior, the split in the long skirt of her dress pushing open to reveal her thigh almost up to the hip.

She heard a gruff intake of breath. And had to tamp down on the desire to escape out of the other side of the vehicle. The cool leather pushed against the backs of her knees through the dress.

'The guy's insatiable in the sack...'

'What if he tries to ravish you?'

Katie's foolish observations came back to haunt her as De Rossi folded his big body into the seat beside her. His wide shoulders filled up the opposite side of the car and made the spacious, luxury black leather interior feel unbearably cramped and claustrophobic.

He leant across her to grasp the seat belt. She pulled back, his face inches from hers, his scent surrounding her. Sandalwood and musk and man. But as his eyes met hers he only smiled again and pulled the seat belt down to click it into place, his knuckles brushing her hip.

'Why are you so skittish, Megan?' he asked.

'I'm just a little nervous, Mr De Rossi,' she blurted out, then glanced around the car searching for a plausible excuse. She was supposed to be flirting with him, making him think she was available for a quick fling, not quaking like someone standing on a fault line. 'About the ball. I don't want to let my father or the company down. It's my first time representing them at such a prestigious event.' Which was actually true; ordinarily that responsibility alone would be reason enough for her nerves.

The warm proprietorial palm settled over her leg, and gave her knee a quick squeeze, touching her again in a way that made her feel owned.

'My name is Dario.' His jaw clenched and she noticed the bunched muscle, twitching. Was it possible she was affecting him as much as he was affecting her?

The thought thrilled her on some visceral level, but disturbed her more.

The possibility of playing him at his own game was almost as terrifying as the endorphins careering through her for the first time in her life.

'We are on a date, remember,' he murmured.

'Thank you for agreeing to escort me,' she said, finally remembering her manners. 'It was nice of you.'

'Nice?' He seemed amused and surprised by the suggestion. 'Not many women have accused me of that.'

She could well imagine. 'My father really appreciated you doing us this favour.' More than De Rossi would ever know. Hopefully.

'There is nothing to appreciate,' he said, cryptically. 'I only do favours when I expect something in return.'

'What do you expect from me?' she said, then realised how suggestive it sounded a moment too late. 'I don't mean...' she stumbled. 'I just...'

'I expect nothing from you, Megan.' He cut into her rambling denials with the skill and precision of a surgeon wielding a scalpel. 'I did this favour for your father.'

Those staggeringly blue eyes studied her, the knowledge in them unnerving her even more. Sensation skittered down her spine, making her breath seize in her lungs, the car's interior now devoid of oxygen. Did he know the real reason her father had asked him to escort her tonight? Was this charade already doomed to failure?

'Don't look so terrified, *cara*,' he said, and she tried to school her features not to give away her fear.

'I promise not to bite. Unless you want me to,' he said, before touching the intercom button to inform the driver to proceed.

Pinpricks rioted over her skin as the car whisked away from the kerb and she imagined those straight white teeth nipping at all her most sensitive places.

She forced a smile, attempting to shake off the sensual fog he seemed to weave around her so effortlessly.

This was going to be the longest night of her life. Her physical reaction to him was too intense, too overwhelming. How was she supposed to survive an evening in his company without telling him every one of her secrets?

CHAPTER TWO

DARIO DE ROSSI WATCHED AS his date finally appeared from the bathroom on the far side of the ballroom. That was the third time in the last hour that she'd deserted him to go to the powder room. And freshen up, as she'd put it.

She didn't need freshening up. Her dewy skin was lightly flushed, the colour riding high on those apple cheeks, on the rare occasions when she'd been close enough for him actually to see her face. And when she wasn't in the powder room, she was engaged in the most vacuous of conversations with everyone but him, her light breathy laughter making every pulse in his body stand on high alert.

She was not what he had expected.

He had known, of course, the second that Lloyd Whittaker had approached him in the club yesterday morning and asked him to escort his daughter to the ball, that the request was part of the man's last-ditch attempt to save his company. The fool had finally realised who was buying up his stock and had probably thought throwing his daughter at Dario would soften the blow. It wouldn't be the first time a business rival had believed that he could manipulate Dario through his enjoyment of the opposite sex—or believed the garbage written about his love life in the tabloids. Giselle's recent hissy fit in *The Post* hadn't helped in that regard.

It also certainly wouldn't be the first time a powerful man had used and degraded a woman he was supposed to love and protect.

The brutal flash of memory had his gut twisting sharply. He took a sip from the bottle of Italian lager the hosts had imported especially for him and waited for the sensation to pass, while he watched Megan Whittaker make her way towards him.

She took the most circuitous route through the crowd, he noted, stopping to talk to a series of her father's acquaintances, every one of whom, Dario observed as his fist plunged into the pocket of his trousers, seemed to think it was okay to look down her cleavage.

The dress—plunging low enough at the neckline to leave not nearly enough to the imagination—had made his heart slam into his throat and dried up every molecule of saliva in his mouth when she'd walked down the hallway of her apartment. And quite literally taken his breath away when she'd eased onto the seat of the limousine and revealed a mile of toned, tanned thigh. Which had to be an optical illusion, because the woman, despite all those impressive curves, didn't even reach to his collarbone in her ice-pick heels.

He downed the last of the beer, and dumped the empty bottle on a passing waiter's tray, deciding that he'd let Megan off the leash long enough.

He'd only agreed to this date out of curiosity. Because he was bored. He'd wanted to see what foolishness Whittaker had planned—especially as he had remembered the daughter from a tedious event a month ago that he'd attended with Giselle. Strangely he had remembered her eyes, that deep intense green had captivated him, but only for a moment, before she'd ducked her head. She'd avoided him for the rest of the evening. So he'd found it amusing that Whittaker had decided to push her into his path to-night. To do what exactly? Seduce him into releasing his stranglehold on a company her old man had been running into the ground for years?

The idea was so preposterous he had been convinced it couldn't actually be true. That such an apparently inexperienced girl should be used for such a purpose seemed beyond even Whittaker's ability to mismanage the situation. But he'd decided to play the scenario out, mostly for his own entertainment. He'd had no date for the ball, Megan Whittaker had already intrigued him, and he would enjoy proving that he was not the barbarian her father obviously assumed him to be. He was perfectly capable of resisting the charms of any woman—even if he hadn't had one in his bed for over a month.

But then his date had surprised him. Stunned him even. And he didn't like to be surprised, much less stunned. She was nervous, yes, and had an artlessness about her, which might have been why he had considered her so inexperienced a month ago, but beneath that was an awareness, a physical response to him that was so intense and unguarded it had done a great deal more than simply captivate or intrigue him.

He didn't like it. He hadn't expected to want her. Or certainly not this much.

But now he had to decide what to do about it.

If Whittaker had sent her on some cock-eyed mission to seduce him, he wasn't about to take advantage of that. But on the other hand, if her response to him was genuine, why shouldn't they enjoy each other for an evening? She couldn't possibly be *that* inexperienced. She was twenty-four, well-travelled, and she'd dated at university in the UK, according to the background check he'd had done by his friend Jared Caine, the owner of Caine Securities.

And he'd felt the way she'd stretched against the palm he'd rested on the slope of her back as they'd left her apartment—like a cat desperate to be stroked.

She wasn't an accomplished flirt, but her instinctive response to a simple touch suggested a rare chemistry. What if she was as wild and vibrant as that russet-coloured hair if he got her into bed?

He hadn't had such a basic reaction to a woman in years, maybe never. He liked sex, he was good at it, but something about Megan had sunk claws into his gut, tearing at his self-control, which he was finding it increasingly difficult to ignore.

He'd sensed her nervousness in the car, so he'd backed off when they'd arrived at the ball, deciding to observe her, and give himself time to figure out what exactly he was supposed to do about the driving need inside him.

But that had obviously been a mistake, because all it was doing was frustrating him more. Truth was, he hadn't expected the avoidance tactics, but as he watched her pause to strike up a conversation with Garson Charters, the senile old judge who seemed to be as fixated on his date's cleavage as every other man in the place, Dario knew that was exactly what her frequent trips to the powder room were about. She was wary of him, not all that surprising if her father had told her to come on to him.

The conniving old bastard probably expected her to wheedle information out of him about their business dealings.

So now he had two choices: he could escort her home, or play with the fire between them regardless of her father's ulterior motives. Whatever happened, though, backing off wasn't an option, because it went against every one of his natural—and a few unnatural—instincts.

He heard the string orchestra in the adjoining ballroom

start up a waltz as he marched through the throng of guests sipping champagne and whispering loudly, and made a beeline for his date.

Her head popped up as he approached, almost as if she had a radar ready to alert her to his presence at a ten-metre radius. Her gaze locked on his for a millisecond and then flicked away, but not before he saw the jolt of awareness cross her features.

Her hunger was as real as his.

She said something to the elderly judge, who still had his beady eyes focused on her cleavage, then began to edge past the guy, heading back towards the bathroom.

No way, not this time.

He caught up with her in a few strides and hooked her wrist, drawing her to a halt. 'Not so fast, *cara*. Where are you going?'

The colour in her cheeks deepened, her eyes widening like those of a startled deer. The smoky perfection of her make-up and the hint of glitter on her eyelids did nothing to mask the unguarded sparkle of awareness in the emerald-green gaze.

'Hi, Dario,' she said breathlessly. 'I think I left something in the restroom.'

'What did you leave in the restroom?'

She scraped her teeth over her full bottom lip, for less than a second, but it sent a shot of heat straight to his crotch.

'Um…my…' She paused, obviously casting around for something.

Unlike her father, she wasn't an accomplished liar.

He stowed the thought. She might be Whittaker's daughter, but he'd seen little evidence this evening of any deviousness on Megan's part. She couldn't even seem to flirt with any degree of sophistication—her desire for him as blatant as her nerves whenever he got within a few feet of her. He could feel the slight tremors in her arm and the pounding beat of her pulse beneath the fingers he had on her wrist.

'Whatever it is, it will be fine in the restroom until after this dance,' he said, linking his fingers with hers as he made his way towards the dance floor in the adjacent ballroom.

She followed behind him as they weaved their way through the crowd, her reluctance palpable. Almost as palpable as the quiver of reaction in her fingers. He clasped her hand harder, not sure why he was seeking to reassure her.

'What dance?' she gasped. The confusion in her voice was almost as much of a turn-on as the tremor in her fingers.

He drew her into the ballroom and swung her into the crowd, deftly joining the other dancers as he lifted her arm high and then placed his other hand at the dip of her waist. 'This dance.'

She matched her steps to his instinctively. He gave her waist a light squeeze, leading her effortlessly into the turn, and dragged her closer. 'Put your hand on my shoulder, Megan,' he ordered, pulling her easily into his body, until the length of her pressed against him from shoulder to hip. Those impressive breasts plumped up against his chest.

She did as she was told.

He swallowed around the renewed jolt of lust, willing his crotch to behave itself. At least until they were off the dance floor and he could get her somewhere private. His decision had been made.

Playing with fire it is, then.

CHAPTER THREE

MEGAN WAS IN TROUBLE. In big, broad, six-foot-three trouble. And she didn't have any viable strategies left to get her out of trouble.

Because her first and only strategy, of hiding in the bathroom until she came up with a better strategy, had just gone down in flames, even though De Rossi had been surprisingly co-operative at first.

But now that strategy had crashed and burned. And she was far too aware of him to come up with another. The deliberate beats of the waltz reverberated in her ears, the sprinkle of light from the chandeliers dazzling her as he swung her around with practised ease.

With his body plastered against hers, she felt overwhelmed by the heat coming off him, the bunch and flex of his shoulder muscles as she clung to the fabric of his tuxedo; and the flare of arousal in his darkened pupils—all proof she wasn't the only one caught in this maelstrom.

His big body surrounded her, his heady scent frying the few functioning brain cells she had left and sending her hormones into meltdown. She could hardly breathe, let alone think.

The hard planes of his chest pressed against her breast as he whisked her round again. And she stumbled. His muscular forearm braced across her back, lifting her off the floor for a beat.

'Steady,' he murmured against her hair as her heels clicked down on the polished parquet. 'Follow my lead.'

She surrendered as he propelled her round the dance floor, past the envious stares of the women around her. He looked magnificent, lean and graceful in the tuxedo but with that air of raw, rugged masculinity that made the other men stand back.

She felt light-headed, her caution and control obliterated under the tractor-beam gaze she'd felt on her all evening, even when she was busy scurrying off to the bathroom for the umpteenth time.

The music swirled around them, the twinkle of light above them as they weaved in and out of the other dancers disorientating her. It was as if she were in the heart of a kaleidoscope, the colour and light dazzling her and leaving her dazed. Every inch of her skin stretched tight over her bones, so that she could feel each millimetre that touched his: the controlling press of his large palm on her hip, the rise and fall of his breathing, slow and steady against her own ragged pants; the thud of her heart, audible above the glide of cello strings marking the beat.

At last the music ended and he came to a halt. She stepped back as he let her go. Grateful for the space, even if his scent still enveloped her.

'You dance very well.' She forced the words out. Wondering if inane chatter might be a viable strategy.

'Do you wish to leave?' he replied.

Obviously not.

'Yes.' The word popped out on a breathless sigh.

He took her hand to lead her off the dance floor. A few people tried to waylay them, but he marched past as if he hadn't noticed. Maybe he hadn't, but she had. She felt as if she had a sign on her forehead—'woman being claimed'.

Her father's suggestion came back to haunt her. He'd wanted her to seduce this man, and she'd agreed to try, but why did what was happening now feel as if it had nothing to do with her father, or Whittaker's, or even rescuing Katie's dreams?

She wanted De Rossi for herself. No one else.

Her pulse battered her collarbone, her fingers clasped tightly in his rough palm, the prickle of awareness shooting all over her body. He paused briefly to pick up their coats from the cloakroom attendant at the entrance to the elaborate Westchester town house where the ball was held.

The chauffeur-driven car was waiting at the kerb as they descended the steps. Megan's heels clicked on the paving stones like gunshots, shooting down the last of her caution and control.

Dario didn't wait for the driver but pulled the door open himself. The dark interior beckoned, but she held back, scared to take the next step.

If she entered the car, this man would be her first real lover. And while that hadn't felt like an event of any significance up to this second, it felt significant now. Obviously this was just lust, some pheromonal trick her body was playing on her. She wasn't a hothead like Katie, and she wasn't a romantic either. She didn't need the conceit of hearts and flowers to justify a purely physical urge. But she'd never had this urge with any other man. And because of that, she couldn't do this thing while there was still so much deception between them.

'Get in the car, Megan,' he murmured, his voice deep with purpose. 'Or I'm liable to do something that is going to get us both arrested.'

She turned to find herself surrounded by him again, his arm braced against the roof of the car, her back flush against the door frame; she could feel the thick ridge touching her belly through their clothing.

'I can't... I have to tell you something first.'

'If it's about your father, and the reason he set up this date, don't bother. I already know.'

'You do?' She pressed a palm to his chest, shock overlaid with bone-deep relief.

The clatter of his heartbeat through the starched linen felt like a validation, silencing the cacophony of objections in her mind. He was as blown away by their chemistry as she was. That was all that mattered, surely? If he knew about her father's plan, this wasn't seedy, or underhand, or unethical. It was nothing more than two healthy adults fulfilling a need.

He nodded, his dark hair shining black in the streetlamp. 'Tell me, are you here for him, for his company, or for me?'

'I...'

For me. I'm here for me.

But even as the truth rang in her head, she couldn't voice it. Paralysed by words whispering across her consciousness from another April night, spiced with the juniper scent of gin and selfishness, the words her mother had whispered to her before she left. The last words her mother had ever spoken to her.

'I have to leave with him, baby. He makes Mummy so happy. Daddy will understand eventually.'

'I... I can't,' she finally blurted out.

She didn't want to be like her mother, she couldn't be. Maybe she had the same biological urges, urges she'd tried to deny for so long, but she couldn't sleep with her father's enemy and do nothing to try to save him.

'Why can't you?' De Rossi asked.

'Because it would kill my father if you destroyed Whittaker's.'

The dark scowl on Dario's face would have been frightening, if she still had some control of her faculties. Instead it only seemed to spike the fire in her blood. Would a man as ruthless in business as Dario consider changing his mind? Would he stop his pursuit of her father's company for her? Did he want her that much?

'I promise you, I have no intention of destroying your father's company.' He ground the words out.

She tried to control the foolish spurt of emotion at the concession. But she couldn't help it. As smart and sensible and grounded as she had always been about life and business, and as aware as she was of De Rossi's ruthlessness, and his cynicism, she was still moved that he would give her this, because she'd asked it of him.

'*Grazie,*' she said.

His brow quirked, then his lips tipped up in a feral smile that should have been terrifying but was instead terrifyingly exciting.

'Don't thank me yet.' He gave her a firm pat on the backside. 'Now get in the car.'

She laughed, she actually laughed, as she scrambled inside. All the stresses and strains of the last twenty-four hours floated off into the Manhattan night as the car sped through the evening traffic towards his home—his love nest—on Central Park West.

Whittaker's would be saved. Her father could stop freaking out about losing the company that had been in their family for generations and she could have this night of erotic exploration with a man who made her blood bubble and fizz beneath her skin, without a single regret.

It took ten minutes to drive through the moonlit park, a few hardy and fearless joggers still peppering the well-

lit streets as they passed Belvedere Castle's fairy-tale tur-
rets. Megan felt almost as fearless as those intrepid joggers
when the car drew to a stop and Dario got out. He hadn't
spoken during the journey, and neither had she. But the
fever of anticipation stirring her blood made her fingers
shake as he helped her out of the car.

'So this is your love nest?' she said.

'My what?' he asked as she tilted her head to take in
the two towers of the art deco building, the ornate and op-
ulent architecture a luxury statement from a bygone era.

But the laugh at his puzzled expression got trapped in
her throat as he escorted her into the building, past the
doorman and a receptionist, until he reached the antique
lift. The intricate iron filigree gates opened as the uni-
formed operator beckoned them inside.

'Good evening, Mr De Rossi.' The man in his late-
fifties tipped his hat at Megan. 'Miss.'

'*Buonasera*, Rick.' Dario's tone was clipped, his hand
gripping hers so tightly she could feel her pulse punching.
'This is Megan Whittaker.'

'Nice to meet you, Rick,' she said, her voice distress-
ingly husky. Heat scorched her neck. How many other late-
night lovers had Rick been introduced to on their way up
to Dario's love nest?

The term felt quaint instead of romantic—which was
for the best, she decided. She wasn't here to make love,
but to have sex for the first time.

Suddenly the enormity of what they were about to do
occurred to her. They hadn't even kissed yet. What would
that firm sensual mouth feel like on hers? How would his
body look naked? She assessed the width of his shoulders
in the perfectly tailored designer coat. He was a well-built
guy; what if all of him was as generously proportioned?
Would it hurt?

Should she tell him she'd never actually gone all the way before?

Her pulse rabbited against her collarbone as she watched the gold arrow above their heads swing in an arc signalling the floors.

Despite the antique design, the lift whisked them up to the twenty-sixth floor without a single creak. Too soon, and yet not soon enough. Dario bid the operator goodnight and led her into a palatial lobby area. Fresh flowers stood on a side table, the only touch of softness against the sleek modern lines.

Shrugging off his coat, he dumped it on an armchair, then lifted her wrap off her shoulders. Despite the warmth pumping out of a central air system, she shivered.

Callused hands settled on her bare shoulders and he turned her to face him.

His handsome face, rigid with desire, should have frightened her, at least a little bit. But somehow it felt compelling, for him to want her so much. His thumbs glided over her collarbone. His fingers curled around her nape with exquisite tenderness. And trapped her in place. Then his lips. Firm, sensual, and unapologetic, slanted across hers, triggering a tsunami of sensation.

Her breath got trapped somewhere around her solar plexus. The hard, unyielding line of his body imprinted itself on her curves, making her want to yield. Instead of demanding or devouring, his lips were coaxing, gentle, until her mouth opened on a huff and his tongue plundered.

He explored, exploited, taking control of the kiss. Shivers of awareness reverberated in her core, then his fingers fisted in her hair to angle her face so he could go deeper, take more. Her heart beat violently against her ribcage, like the wings of a trapped bird trying to escape. She plastered herself against him, absorbing the heat of his body, and kissed him back, her tongue darting out to duel with his. The sudden feeling of weightlessness was as terrifying as the desperate flare of longing, the shocking well of desire surging up her torso to obliterate everything but the sight, the sound, the taste of him. Earthy and raw and so staggeringly real.

The kiss could only have lasted for a few moments, but still she staggered, unsteady on her feet, when he lifted his head abruptly. His brows lifted, his eyes flaring hot, and she wondered for a second if he were as stunned as she was by the intensity of feeling that had passed between them.

Taking her hand, he led her down the corridor and into a huge, double-height room. A majestic sweep of stairs led to a mezzanine level, the deep leather sofas along the back wall the only furnishings. Huge floor-to-ceiling leaded windows looked out over the dark expanse of Central Park, the lake and the twinkle of lights from the East Side skyline beyond.

She could see her own reflection in the mullioned glass, her breath heaving in and out, her satin curves shimmering in the light from the hallway as he stood behind her. He glided his thumbs under the gown's diamanté straps.

'Yes?' The low question shattered the silence.

'Yes,' she managed around the thickening in her throat.

He eased the straps over her shoulder blades. The rasp of the gown's zip seemed deafening. Satin caught at her waist, and then slid down to pool around her feet, revealing the lacy royal-blue lingerie Annalise had insisted on buying to go with the gown.

Her breath hitched painfully as she heard the click of her bra releasing. He dragged the lace straps off her shoulders to slide down her arms. Her heavy breasts were released from their confinement. His lips caressed her neck, suckling on the pulse point as his hands covered the swollen mounds, his fingers circling her nipples.

Sensation tugged at her sex as he rolled the rigid peaks between thumb and forefinger, plucking then squeezing. Her knees went liquid, and a strong arm banded around her waist to hold her up. Her pale flesh shone white against his darkness.

His lips caressed the side of her neck as he growled. 'I can't wait any longer to have you.'

She pulled away and turned to face him. Her pulse was going berserk. She dragged a precious lungful of air into her lungs and tasted him, the subtle aroma of sandalwood and clean laundry detergent.

His thumb skimmed her cheek. The gentle touch had all her nerve-endings springing to high alert.

No man had ever looked at her with such hunger in his eyes. She absorbed the heat and intensity and it felt like a benediction, a celebration of everything she was that she had always been terrified to admit to.

The heat between her legs melted into a puddle of need, making her skin sensitive and her senses alert to the scent and taste of him, the rough sound of his breathing.

She squeezed her thighs together. 'Neither can I,' she said.

Dario stared at the girl in front of him—an artless seductress whose acute awareness of his touch had been torturing him all evening.

He had become spellbound by his own lust. He'd never wanted a woman this much, so much he wasn't sure he could be gentle—and that frightened him. He could actually read every one of her emotions as they flitted across her face, her attempts to wrestle them under control almost as bewitching as the hard peaks of her breasts, which begged for his mouth.

Need coiled hard in his gut, the pounding in his crotch unbearable.

He cupped her breast. She jolted but didn't draw away.

'Are you sure, *cara*?' He wanted no lies or obligations between them. He'd promised not to destroy her father's company. But it had never been his intention to destroy it, only to take it from the man...tonight, when the final deal with the last of Whittaker's shareholders went through at midnight.

'Yes,' she murmured.

He threaded his fingers in her hair, loosening the up-do. As the soft, silky strands teased his fingertips, her scent curled around him, fresh and vivid, and heat powered through his body. Her eyes widened, her breathing coming in harsh pants now. And he knew she felt it too, that tug of yearning, the driving need to finish what they'd started.

Her teeth sank into her bottom lip, mesmerising him, and calling to every one of his baser instincts, instincts he'd spent a lifetime trying to control.

Need overwhelmed him as he lifted her into his arms. Placing her on the couch, he lowered his head, unable to resist the pull of that lush mouth a moment longer.

He heard the soft gasp, tasted her excitement and her trepidation. It could only be a trick of the night, this veneer of innocence. No woman could be innocent and drive him this insane, but even so he enjoyed the challenge as he coaxed and cajoled, tempting her with his tongue.

Her lips opened at last on a shuddering sigh. His tongue swept into her mouth, exploring. Then she began to explore back. Tentative at first, then bold. Matching his hunger with her own. Driving them both mad. She tasted glorious, sweet and eager and new.

Her fingers glided beneath his jacket to cling to his waist. Heat slammed into him. He lifted himself up, yanking off his jacket and flinging it on the floor, pressing her back into the cool leather. Lifting her hands above her head, he bracketed her wrists in one hand to palm the pouting tip of her breast.

The nipple poked against his palm, standing proud as she arched her back, her breathing coming in desperate gasps as she pressed into the caress. He circled the tight bud, all thoughts of caution obliterated by her seductive response.

He trapped the peak between his teeth, tonguing it and then sucking it into his mouth. She sobbed something incoherent in the darkness, the desire in her voice rasping across his skin and sending the need spiralling out of control.

He wanted her, more than he'd wanted any woman, her artless response tapping into some primal desire to claim her, brand her, devour her.

'Please, I can't...' She jolted against him.

'Shh...' he crooned, desperate to relieve the throbbing ache in his crotch. She wanted him just as much. He could feel it in her body, which was tight as a bowstring, and in the staggered rise and fall of her breathing; he could see it in the flush of arousal spreading across the delicate skin of her collarbone.

'That feels so good—' Her voice choked off as he sucked the nipple against the roof of his mouth, tugging hard. She jerked against his hold, and pulled her hands free to plunge them into his hair.

The thin thread on his control snapped, primal desire charging through his system. Damn thought and sense and reason and anything that would stop him from making her come apart in his arms.

The madness to have her consumed him. He inhaled the delicate floral fragrance, like a narcotic drug. Pressing the heel of his palm between her thighs, to test her readiness, he felt her warm and wet through the lace. She quaked with need, daring him to take her, claim her, control her. Here. Now. And satisfy the need driving them both insane.

He plunged beneath the damp fabric of her panties, circling the tight bud. She cried out, bucking against the intimate touch. But the slick folds told a different story. She needed this. Needed him.

Ripping her panties, he grasped her thighs, spreading them wide to press the aching ridge against her centre.

'Let me have you,' he growled, the ferocity of the demand foreign to his own ears.

She looked dazed, her eyes unfocused, but she dropped her head in the tiniest hint of a nod.

The madness took over. He grappled with his zip and released his erection, then, positioning himself against the swollen folds, he thrust hard.

But as he surged deep, he heard the cry of pain against his neck, felt the tiny barrier, before she tightened on him like a fist.

He stopped dead.

He was buried to the hilt, the orgasm already licking at the base of his spine. But the hot clasp of her body was so tight. Too tight.

'What the...?' He swore viciously, shocked and sickened by the evidence of her innocence. 'You are a virgin?' he said, the shock only countered by the fierce unstoppable desire to move, to finish.

Megan buried her face in his neck, her whole body reeling from the shocking invasion. It had been so good, so bright, so beautiful, but now she felt impaled. He was too big, filling up every space inside her, all those empty places that had ached for so long.

She stiffened as he shifted, the thick heat branding her insides, stroking a place so deep inside, it spun her mind away from coherent thought again and back towards that glorious heat that had consumed her just moments ago.

'*Cara...*' He cradled her cheek. 'Answer me. Why you did not tell me I am...your first?' His perfect English seemed to have deserted him, the words clumsy, those deep blue eyes alive with stunned disbelief and raw aching need.

'I'm sorry,' she said, not sure why she was apologising, but he looked so horrified, she didn't know what else to say.

He held her hips, easing back, withdrawing that glorious heat. She gripped his buttocks, felt the muscles jump.

'Don't stop. It doesn't matter, really it doesn't. And it feels good.' It didn't exactly; it felt sore, and overwhelming.

'I don't want to hurt you.' He bit out the words, torn between temper and what sounded like torment.

Why did this matter to him so much? She wanted to ask.

But what she wanted more was for the bright, beautiful feeling to return. So that she felt empowered and special, not crushed and broken.

'I'm not fragile. I won't break,' she said, determined to make him believe it.

He swore softly in Italian, his fingers holding her thighs, poised at her entrance. 'Are you sure?' he asked.

She nodded, unbearably moved by the torment in his voice. 'Yes, I'm sure.'

He sank back into her to the hilt.

Her breath clogged in her throat. She could feel him everywhere, the stretching feeling unbearable again, but with it came the swift surge of pleasure as he nudged a place deep inside. He rocked his hips, and nudged it again.

'Si sente bene?' he asked, his English apparently having deserted him entirely.

'Yes, it feels good,' she said as the pleasure began to build in fierce undulating waves, sweeping away the pain, the confusion, until all that was left was the glorious swell of ecstasy, pure and perfect. The sensitive tips of her breasts rubbed against the hard contours of his chest through his linen shirt, sending arrows of sensation surging into her sex.

The slick sounds of their bodies slapping together, the scent of pheromones and sweat heavy on the air, the soft bump of her spine against the leather, faded into the background until all she could hear were the pants of her breathing and the grunts of his. He established a punishing rhythm, forceful, relentless, unstoppable. Then reached between them to press his thumb to the heart of her.

The huge wave crested, her whole being now focused on the burning core of her body, clambering for release.

She held on to him, terrified, frantic and overjoyed, all at the same time. He grew to impossible proportions inside her, his thrusts jerky and uncoordinated in their desperation.

She rode on that high wide plane between intense pleasure and unbearable pain for what seemed like an eternity, but could only have lasted a heartbeat. And her body soared.

Her thin cry cut the still air as the wave crashed over her, overwhelming in its intensity, and his shout of release echoed in her ear, the hot seed searing her insides.

What the hell just happened?

Sensation came back in small increments as Dario waited for his heart to stop battering his ribs like a wild stallion trying to kick its way to freedom.

The sultry scent of orange blossoms and sweat, the weight of her hands on his waist, the clinging cotton of the shirt he hadn't bothered to take off. The tight clasp of her surrounding him as the iron-hard erection finally began to soften and the ache in his groin subsided.

He buried his face against her neck, the soft skin damp and fragrant, and felt the hummingbird flutter of her pulse, as wild and erratic as his own.

He couldn't move, didn't want to move, grateful for the shadowy light as they lay cocooned together on the couch.

He'd had good sex before. Hell, he'd had spectacular sex before. He'd never had sex like that before, or an orgasm so intense it had felt as if it were ripping out a part of his soul.

Who is this woman? And what has she done to me?

He eased up on his elbows and felt her flinch beneath him. The sob of discomfort whispered against his face, making shame twist in his gut.

She had been innocent, and he'd ravished her like a man possessed. Not only that, but he had taken her without protection. Spilled his seed inside her. He should have stopped, withdrawn, but she had transfixed him somehow. And he had been unable to focus on anything but her. And the need to possess her.

Why hadn't she told him? She should have told him she was a virgin. He would never have—

Stop lying to yourself.

No force on earth would have stopped him, once she had given him her consent and unleashed the wild hunger inside him.

He climbed off her, careful not to jostle her. He couldn't make out her expression in the shadowy light, but he could see the tremors raking her body.

Lush and lovely, her pale skin looked somehow ethereal

in the soft glow of light from the lobby. He felt the renewed stirring of desire, and shame mixed with anger in his gut.

You are not an animal.

The admonition seemed like another lie though as he zipped his trousers and walked to pick up the jacket he had discarded. He returned to the couch to find her seated, her arms wrapped around her waist. He laid the jacket over her shoulders, and drew her close under his arm.

'Why are you shivering? Are you cold?' he asked, his voice hoarse.

She had to be sore, but was she also scared of him?

He tucked a riotous curl behind her ear, relief assailing him when she turned to him and smiled. The urge to kiss her gripped him again at the guileless tilt of her lips.

He resisted it. Not a good idea, given that kissing her would lead to other, more dangerous pursuits.

'No, I'm not cold. I just… I think it's a reaction…' She hesitated, biting down on that full bottom lip that had driven him wild, was still driving him wild. He forced himself to look away from her mouth.

'A reaction to what?' he prompted, determined to distract them both with conversation. He didn't usually like to talk much after sex, but this was different. He'd never been a woman's first before. It wasn't a responsibility he wanted or would have chosen, but he felt it nonetheless.

'A reaction to…' She hesitated again, but she didn't look embarrassed or unsure, just as if she were searching for the right words. 'Well, the orgasm, I guess. It was pretty intense. You're much better than my vibrator.'

The chuckle rumbled up from his chest, part amusement, part desire, but mostly relief. Her blunt honesty was ridiculously charming, especially when she blushed.

'*Grazie*, that is quite a compliment,' he murmured.

She gave a shy smile, looking embarrassed now but also amused. 'Sorry, I'm not very good at this.'

He looped the wayward curl behind her ear again, let his thumb linger on the smooth skin of her jaw, the laughter dying on his lips. 'On the contrary, you are very good at it, especially for someone with so little practice.'

The blush climbed up to her hairline, but she seemed pleased with the compliment. He felt a strange sensation in his chest and dropped his hand. What was he doing? Behaving like a besotted fool, when he needed to make sure that there would be no fallout from his irresponsible behaviour.

'Megan, we must talk about practicalities.'

'What practicalities?' she said, the guileless expression making him feel uneasy. Could anyone really be this innocent? Was this whole scenario some kind of set-up? Had Whittaker been devious enough to offer up his virgin daughter as a means of trapping him?

'I did not use a condom,' he said bluntly. 'Are you on the pill?'

The flush fired across her cheeks and her eyes widened. Either she was an actress worthy of an award, or the shocked reaction was not faked.

'No, I'm not, I'm sorry, I didn't—'

'There is no need for apologies.' He cut off her stumbling words, feeling oddly ashamed at the cynical direction of his thoughts.

Megan Whittaker was that rare thing, a person as genuine as they appeared to be—just as he had originally suspected.

'We are both responsible for the error,' he added. 'I am clean, I have a regular check-up and testing for my company insurance—and I never usually have sex without protection,' he continued, suspecting the threat of disease was probably the reason for her horrified reaction. His conquests after all had been well documented in the press, and made to seem much more indiscriminate than they actually were. Because, until Megan, he had always chosen his sexual partners with exquisite care. Which was precisely why he had never found himself in this position before. 'If you need proof,' he said, when she didn't respond, 'I can get my doctor to contact you.'

'No, that's not necessary. I trust you,' she said, marking out her innocence even more. He wanted to tell her not to trust him, not to trust any man, but before he could find the words she added, 'I don't either, by the way... Have sex without protection, I mean. Just in case you were wondering, and were worried too.'

The gauche statement was so earnest, his lips tipped up in a wry smile. 'With your vibrator, you mean?'

'Um, well...' The blush intensified on her cheeks, before she buried her hands in her face and groaned. 'Oh, God, I feel like such a clueless muppet.'

'Not at all, *piccola*.' He laughed, he couldn't help it; her found her reaction charming. 'We do still have one problem though,' he said, sobering. 'When did you have your last period?'

'Oh, I...' She raised her face, the blush still burning brightly. 'About a week ago. I think.'

'Then we are not quite in the middle of your cycle,' he said. 'But you should take emergency contraception. Yes? As a precaution.' He watched her intently for her reaction to the request, his anger at himself increasing. What would he do if she refused?

'Yes, yes, of course. I'll go to a pharmacy.' She jumped up from the couch, her panicked reaction easing the tension in his gut. 'I better go now. I'll need to find an all-night pharmacy. I don't even know if you can buy it across the counter.'

'Megan, there is no need to panic.' He rose from the couch too and tucked a knuckle under her chin. Raising her face to his, he touched his thumb to her mouth, the heat powering through him surprising him. 'And stop biting your lip. Or I will not be responsible for the consequences.'

She released her lip instinctively. 'But I should go, Dario. I need to get the contraception. I don't want…'

'You have up to a week to take it.'

'I do?'

'I believe so. Don't look at me like that, *piccola*.' He smiled again, captivated once more by how easily she was to read. 'I promise you, I don't make a habit of making love without contraception.' The truth was he had never made this mistake before, even as an untried boy, but she didn't need to know that. 'But I am a cautious man.' Or he had been until now. 'As I have no desire to father a child.'

'Yes, of course.' She nodded, her cheeks still as bright as beacons. 'I'm sorry, I'm making a hash of this, aren't I?'

'Not at all. This is new to you, I understand.'

She shuddered slightly, his tux jacket dwarfing her as she tucked her arms into the sleeves and held it close. 'I should probably leave now anyway though. I'll make sure I go to a pharmacy first thing in the morning.'

She was correct, of course, this had just been a chance for them to slake the lust that had sparked between them as soon as they had met.

But as she stood before him, beautiful and beguiling in the half light, he knew the spark hadn't yet been extinguished. And tonight would be their only opportunity, because he would not be contacting her again.

In a few hours, his agents would complete the hostile

takeover of her father's company, giving their encounter a one-night embargo.

It was of course dishonest of him not to clarify his earlier statement about Whittaker's, so there could be no confusion about what he'd meant. But he didn't mix business with pleasure. And for that reason, he did not feel guilty for giving her the cryptic answer he had. What happened in the boardroom had no bearing on relations in the bedroom—or rather the couch. What had passed between them, however wild and uncontrolled, could never be more than a physical attachment after all.

Once she discovered the truth, she would be upset. She might even feel he had got her here under false pretences. After all, his reply to her request had been deliberately ambiguous. But as his gaze drifted down her bare legs and he remembered the sweet shudder of her release, the feel of her thighs clasping his hips as she came, he knew he didn't want their one night to end so soon.

In fact, he almost felt regretful that she would no doubt hate him in the morning.

She picked her gown up from the floor and clasped it to her chest. 'Is there somewhere I could wash up,' she said, looking shy again and unsure.

He walked over to her, his mind made up. They would have this night.

He would show her the finesse, the reverence he had failed to show her so far. She deserved better than a frantic romp on a couch. He wasn't a romantic or a sentimental man, but he was a good lover.

The last of the shame drained away. He could keep the wildness in check; he would not ravish her again.

'There is no need to leave,' he said, tugging the cool satin out of her hands.

'But I...'

He placed a finger on her lips. 'No buts. We have all night. Why not let me show you all the other things your vibrator cannot do for you?'

The blush intensified, and he found the lightness, the laughter threatening to roll up his torso again. Not a response he was used to when in the process of seducing a beautiful woman.

No wonder this woman was so damn captivating. She was simply the opposite of his usual type. Her uniqueness would wear thin quickly enough, but he was enjoying himself for now. And he planned to enjoy himself a lot more tonight. While making sure Megan enjoyed herself too, of course. She might hate him in the morning, but eventually she would thank him for showing her that sex was much more enjoyable when not compromised by emotional entanglements.

'I'm not sure that's a good idea,' she said.

'Why not?' He cradled her cheek, enjoying the way she leant into his palm instinctively. And her pupils darkened dramatically. Did she know he could see exactly how much she wanted him?

'Because, to be perfectly honest, I'm a little sore.'

The delightfully gauche statement, delivered with complete sincerity, had him throwing back his head and laughing out loud for the first time in longer than he could remember.

'What's so funny?' she asked, grumpily.

He scooped her up into his arms.

She grabbed hold of his neck, her frown of protest only making him laugh harder as he headed to the stairs and the deluxe king-size bed and lake-size bath with power shower he planned to make good use of in the next few hours.

He placed a kiss on her forehead, enjoying the feel of

her bottom against his forearm. Why not keep her naked and wanting the rest of the night?

Why had he never considered before how arousing it would be to help a woman discover the frontiers of her own pleasure?

'Do not look so worried, *cara mia*,' he said as he took the stairs two at a time. 'There are many ways to make love, not all of them require penetration. Clearly your vibrator does not help with this either.'

'I wish I'd never told you about my vibrator,' she said. 'Now you're never going to stop making fun of me.'

'I am not making fun,' he said, although of course he was. 'But I do intend to remedy the situation. With your permission?'

She huffed out a breath, but the excitement and arousal dancing in her eyes told a different story, especially when she tightened her grip on his neck and said, with mock severity, 'Oh, all right, then—if you insist.'

CHAPTER FOUR

Didn't the man ever eat?

Megan stared at the dazzlingly clean and startlingly empty shelves in the huge double wide fridge. Apart from a couple of bottles of pricey mineral water, a bottle of expensive champagne, some imported Italian lager, some milk and an untouched box of expensive chocolates, there was nothing to eat. She searched the cupboards a second time. Nope, still nothing there except some strong Italian coffee.

She turned in a circle. The oversized Italian football shirt she'd fished out of a drawer in Dario's walk-in closet skimmed her bare thighs as she took in the acres of granite and polished steel. The tingle of sensation as the material brushed her nipples had a memory flushing through her. Of Dario ravishing her breasts in the shower.

Moving swiftly on.

She concentrated on the sun, which had begun to climb over Central Park, shining off the lake and adding to that magnificent view. She'd woken up with Dario's big body wrapped around hers in sleep. He'd tucked her against his chest after he'd brought her to a stunning orgasm for the fourth time in one night... She lifted the glass of mineral water she'd poured herself from the meagre supplies in the fridge and took several gulps to ease the dryness in her throat.

Dario De Rossi a snuggler. Who'd have thought it?

She smiled to herself, feeling a little giddy. It was a Saturday, so she didn't need to go to work today. She knew her father would want her to call him to confirm if she had discovered anything, but there would be no need for that now. Dario had told her he wasn't going to go after Whittaker's. Maybe he had never intended to.

But unlike last night, she didn't feel the need to run off and hide. He'd been so solicitous after they'd made love that first time. And so devoted for the rest of the night. He'd soaked with her in the bathtub, then done things to her body that had proved that, yes, vibrators could not replace a flesh-and-blood man.

The sex had been hot, intense and unbelievably intimate. But she had adored every minute of it. Was this what her mother had been so addicted to? Now she understood. Something fluttered in her chest. Something sweet and seductive and more than a little bit silly.

She set about figuring out the state-of-the-art coffee maker and ignored the feeling. Their liaison was unlikely to last past this morning—so there was no point in getting carried away. She needed to be pragmatic. Really, she ought to be heading home. She had to find a pharmacy en route and take care of the practicalities—as Dario had put it. Her cheeks heated as she recalled their excruciating conversation from the night before. Her hand strayed to her belly. And she wondered, just for a split second, what it would be like to have the child of a man like Dario De Rossi.

Not going there.

She shook off the foolish, fanciful thoughts and let her hand drop.

She didn't want Dario's baby. She didn't want anyone's baby. She was fairly sure she wasn't cut out for mother-

hood, any more than her own mother had been. And if by
chance Dario's seed had found fertile ground last night,
she would remedy the problem as soon as she got back
home. But first she needed coffee.

She concentrated on filling the machine's in-built
grinder with coffee beans. It didn't take long to have the
strong, chicory scent filling up the kitchen. If only she had
more clothing, she could pop out and get something for
breakfast. She liked to cook. And she felt she owed Dario.
He'd made last night magnificent. And she hadn't exactly
held up her end, so to speak. She frowned as she poured
a steaming cup of coffee into one of the demi-cups in the
cupboard. He'd been so controlled, so focused, it had been
flattering and exhausting and beyond amazing. But somehow the times after that first time hadn't felt quite as, well,
quite as equal. She'd felt oddly like a pupil, being played
by a master. Her attempts to touch him, to caress him, to
drive him crazy back, rebuffed.

'I'm impressed.'

She jerked round, sloshing hot coffee over the counter,
to find Dario standing behind her, his broad, muscular
chest making her pulse race. He wore a pair of sweat pants
low on his hips—revealing the most mouthwatering V she
had ever seen in her life—and nothing else. His olive skin
was deeply tanned, even down to the line of his low-rid-
ing pants. His dark hair stood up in clumps on one side of
his head, but unlike her hair—which probably resembled
Frizz City this morning—the rumpled, just-out-of-bed
look only made him sexier. Add that to the jaw sporting
a five o'clock shadow that had given her whisker burn in
some interesting places last night, and the man wouldn't
have looked out of place in a million-dollar cologne ad.

'Still skittish, Megan?' His sensual lips tipped up on
one side in a boyish smile as he leant past her to pour

himself a mug of coffee and the giddy feeling in her chest fluttered again.

She breathed in his scent, the sandalwood aroma a brutal reminder of everything they'd got up to together in the shower.

'You have a habit of creeping up on me,' she said in her defence, but she smiled. Had she actually spent all night in this man's arms? This god among men? No fair.

He laughed, that deep rusty chuckle that had enthralled her last night, when she'd had the oddest sensation that he didn't laugh nearly often enough. It had made her feel special. When she knew she wasn't. But still.

'Why do I impress you?' she asked, shamelessly fishing for a compliment.

The tanned skin around his eyes crinkled, as if he knew exactly what she was up to. 'You figured out the espresso machine without an hour-long tutorial.'

She laughed and glanced back at the complex contraption. 'It's not that hard for a computer geek.'

He sipped his coffee, hummed low in his throat, the sound sending the familiar pinpricks darting down to her sex. Heavens, she was a hopeless case.

'Sexy and smart *and* a great coffee maker.' He leant down to kiss her, the teasing licks sending her senses reeling, his rich coffee taste making the hunger in her gut intensify. But as she opened her mouth to take him in, he pulled back.

'Damn, what do you do to me, *piccola*?'
Little one.

He'd used the same endearment last night. It was probably something he called all the women who slept with him. It didn't make her special or different—she needed to remember that. But even so, the deep blue of his irises seemed to sparkle just for her when he said it. This playful, provocative side of him made her feel as if she was getting a glimpse of something he never showed to anyone else.

'Nothing you don't do to me,' she replied, because it was true.

'Hmm, I doubt that,' he said enigmatically, before he walked round and perched on one of the bar stools by the kitchen counter.

'I thought I could cook us breakfast, before I go,' she said, trying not to sound too eager. 'But you don't have any food.'

'I use a caterer when I entertain. Otherwise I eat out.'

'I see.' Although she didn't really. Surely for any house to be a home, you had to eat in occasionally? 'Well, I guess I should be going, then.'

'There is no need to leave yet. I can get groceries sent up. I like the idea of you cooking me breakfast.' He glanced at her shirt. 'Especially in my Roma shirt. Maybe I will ravish you afterwards on the countertop.'

The arrogantly male statement and the wicked intention in his eyes should have unsettled her, but instead it only excited her. But then every damn thing about the man turned her on.

'If you're going to be a caveman about it, I may have to rescind my offer,' she teased back.

'We will have to see if I can persuade you,' he said and she knew she was sunk. They both knew her resistance when it came to him was zero. 'How much time do you have?' he asked.

She glanced at the clock on the glass wall next to the eight-ring cooker…that he never used. And blinked, shocked to realise it was inching towards ten o'clock. She had to get back to her apartment before Katie woke up. Katie was not an early riser on a Saturday when she didn't have to go to college, thank goodness. But she didn't want her sister asking probing questions about where she'd been all night. And she definitely didn't want her finding out about the morning-after pill debacle—which meant making sure she bought it and took it before Katie got out of bed.

'I didn't realise it was so late,' she said, unable to keep the regret from her voice. 'I really need to go home and change and handle the other…um…practicalities we talked about last night.'

'This is a shame,' he said, and seemed to mean it— which didn't help with the giddy flutter in her chest.

But then her phone buzzed on the counter. She picked it up. A message from her father.

What the hell happened with De Rossi last night?

Guilt washed over her as she glanced up at Dario. Her father sounded as if he was freaking out again. This couldn't be right. Dario had told her he wasn't pursuing Whittaker's, that there would be no takeover.

'I should probably take this,' she said.

A strange chill settled in her stomach as she walked to the other side of the room and texted her father back.

Don't panic Dad, everything's okay. Dario assured me he's not attempting a takeover. I spoke to him.

She stared at the text, then quickly scrolled back to delete Dario and replace it with Mr De Rossi. Then she pressed send. She'd done a lot more than speak to Dario, but her father did not need to know that. Their liaison had nothing to do with the company. Not now.

The reply came back within seconds. And the sinking

feeling in her stomach became a black hole. The vicious words felt like a punch in the gut she couldn't defend herself against.

Stupid little slut! You slept with him, didn't you? After he stole my company. You're no better than your bitch of a mother.

'He shouldn't say such things to you.'

She swung round to find Dario watching her, his expression grim. She whipped the phone behind her back, humiliated and sick at the same time. Had he read that?

'He's upset. I think… He's under a lot of stress at the moment,' she said, instantly jumping to her father's defence. He didn't mean to be cruel. He wasn't a bad man, just an extremely stressed one. 'But I should go, and explain things to him. He's obviously got the wrong end of the stick. He thinks De Rossi Corp is involved in a hostile takeover. And obviously that's not the case, because you promised me yesterday you have no interest in Whittaker's.'

Dario took the phone from her and grasped her hand to lead her to one of the kitchen stools. 'Sit down, Megan. I need to explain something.'

She sat down. Confused now and wary. Why did Dario look so serious? Where had the sexy man of a moment ago gone to? The man who had worshipped her with his mouth, his hands, his body, last night? And why had her father texted her so viciously? None of it made any sense. The company wasn't under threat; it had all been a misunderstanding of some sort.

'Megan, you must understand, I never mix business with pleasure.'

'I know. I'm sorry, I shouldn't have brought it up, it's just he texted me and I—'

'You misunderstand me.'

'Sorry?'

'Last night was about us enjoying each other, not about your father, or his company.'

'I know that, but you promised me that—'

'What I promised you was that I would not destroy Whittaker's. That is what you asked me and I answered truthfully.'

'I know, and that's good.'

'I have no plans to destroy it. Because, as of last night, I now own it.'

She blinked rapidly, the black hole in her stomach opening into a huge pit. A huge gaping pit full of vipers. As he continued to speak in that calm, pragmatic voice, his words became barely audible above the hissing in her head.

'Whittaker's is still a viable company with the right management. It is a heritage brand with excellent prospects. The right management, though, is not your father. E-commerce is the way forward. He has refused to develop that side of the business to any great degree. I only asset-strip companies that have no future.'

He had taken the company away from her father.

He hadn't lied, but he had been economical with the truth. And she'd fallen for it. Because she'd wanted to. She'd heard what she'd wanted to hear in his qualified denial, because she'd wanted him. Her father had every right to call her a slut. Because that was exactly what she was. She'd put her own pleasure above the good of the company. The good of the family. Just like her mother.

Tears stung her eyes, making her sinuses throb. She wouldn't cry. She didn't deserve that indulgence. She had to get back to her apartment, get changed and then go to

see her father and try to make this right. She and Katie
had the money from their mother's trust fund, but her father administered it. He was bound to withdraw Katie's tuition now, to punish Megan for this folly. For this betrayal.

She sniffed, struggling to pull herself together, to ignore the hollow ache in her gut. The same sick feeling that
had paralysed her the night her mother had left, when she
was convinced her mother's departure was somehow her
fault, because she hadn't been a good enough daughter.

She clambered off the stool, but as she tried to walk past
Dario he held her arm, and pulled her round to face him.
'If you are angry with me, you should say so.'

'I'm not angry with you. I'm angry with myself. I've
betrayed a man I love and now I have to tell him what I've
done and hope he doesn't hate me.'

'Why would you love a man who speaks to you like
that?' He sounded annoyed. She didn't understand.

'Please, I have to go.' She tugged out of his grip, and
rushed over to pick up her gown. She would have to wear
it home. The walk of shame really did not get any worse
than this.

'He doesn't deserve your loyalty,' he said, the cynical
edge in his voice cutting through the last of her defences.
'No man does who would use you in such a way.'

But you used me, too.

She pushed the self-pitying thought to one side. Dario
hadn't used her, he had taken what she had offered freely.
But even so, she couldn't bear to look at him as she took
off his football shirt and slipped into the satin sheath. She
should have been embarrassed that he was watching her.
That having those eyes on her, cool and blue and full of
heat, still aroused her. But she was way past embarrass-
ment—everything she had ever known or believed about
herself and her own integrity ripped to shreds.

She deserved her father's scorn.

'We slept together,' she said, pushing her feet into the torturous heels. 'I made a choice to sleep with you. It was the wrong choice. I see that now. I let what I wanted get in the way of what was right.'

Not only that, but she'd allowed herself to believe that a man as ruthless as Dario would put his desire for her above a business deal.

She wasn't just a clueless muppet. She was a hopelessly naïve and narcissistic clueless muppet.

'Don't be foolish,' he demanded. 'This isn't about right or wrong. Or you and me and what we did together last night. This is about your father and his inability to run a company competently. The two circumstances are not related.'

'They are to me.' She picked the wrap up from the floor of the living room and took one last glance at the wide green canopy of Central Park. There would be families down there, on this bright spring day. Families who loved and respected each other. But her father would never respect her again. She'd failed him. Failed herself. Thanks to her hunger for a man who was so far out of her league it was ridiculous.

He snagged her arm again. 'This is madness, Megan. We satisfied a perfectly natural urge last night. Nothing more. There is no need to punish yourself.'

She shook her arm free, blinking furiously to stop the tears from falling—because she would feel even more wretched if he ever found out the truth.

That somehow during their wild night together, she had come to believe she and Dario were doing more than just satisfying a perfectly natural urge.

'I have to go.'

She rushed down the long corridor towards the door,

pathetically grateful he didn't try to stop her. The sound of her heels clicking on the inlaid wood flooring mocked her. Along with the scattershot beats of her heart. And the nausea rolling in her belly.

As she took the lift down, she felt sick at her own stupidity.

But as the cab drove away from the art deco apartment building, she also felt a strange sense of pity. For Dario.

Because for all his wealth and power, for all his good looks and potent sex appeal, his indomitable confidence and charisma, it was clear he did not understand the importance of family.

CHAPTER FIVE

'MEG, WHERE HAVE YOU BEEN?' Katie pounced on her forty minutes later as she let herself into their apartment.

'Oh. My. God. You spent the night with him, didn't you?' Katie hissed as she took in the creased satin gown, the haphazard wrap, and the hastily knotted bundle of frizz on Megan's head. 'Sheesh, is that whisker burn on your cheek?'

Megan placed a hand over the raw skin, ashamed all over again. 'I can't talk about it now.' *Or ever.*

Her head hurt, the deep ache matched by the smarting pain in her tear ducts from the disastrous end to her wild night with Dario De Rossi—and all the tears she refused to shed.

That was nothing though compared to what the company would face now. She would lose her job, and she'd deserve it. A part of her—the small, sane part of her that could still think straight—had reasoned that it wasn't her fault De Rossi had targeted Whittaker's, or that her father's wild scheme to discover Dario's intentions through some sort of computer hack wouldn't have made a difference. But even so, she felt unbearably guilty. For sleeping with a man who had destroyed what her family had spent years building.

'Actually, you don't have to talk about it, I already

know...' Katie grabbed her hand, and tugged her into the alcove off the hallway. 'Dad's here, and he's behaving like a lunatic. He called you all sorts of horrid names and dismissed Lydia. Just sacked her on the spot.'

'Oh, no.' Was Lydia going to be made to pay for her mistakes too?

'Did he say anything about your tuition?' Megan asked, praying that she might be able to limit at least some of the damage.

'Yeah, he's pulling the plug on that. You could have told me he was paying for it,' her sister said, but she didn't look nearly as devastated as Megan had expected.

'Don't worry, Katie, I'll find a way to fund it.' Somehow.

'Forget it, I'll figure out a way to fund it myself,' Katie said dismissively. 'Believe me, that's the least of our worries. We have to deal with Dad first. I think he's lost his marbles. I'm not kidding. He's been ranting and raving about Mum, and you and De Rossi. He's behaving like King Lear on a bender. I think he's on something. He's dangerous.'

'What?' The vice around Megan's temples tightened.

'I tried to call you, to warn you.' Katie's head swivelled round to peek past the column that edged the hallway and gave her a direct view of the living-room door. 'But I kept getting the answer-machine.'

Because Megan had switched off the phone when she'd left Dario's—too much of a coward to bear her father's wrath before she had to. She'd delayed the inevitable still further by stopping at a pharmacy en route. But the chemist's judgmental look as she'd bought the emergency contraception in a crumpled satin ball gown had been more than enough of a guilt trip to remind her of all her transgressions.

'Don't worry,' Megan murmured wearily. She really didn't need Katie's ongoing battle with their father resurfacing and turning this crisis into a catastrophe. 'Dad's mad with me, that's all. I did something he may never forgive me for...' Just the thought of that had the guilt clawing at her insides like a rabid dog. 'He's lost Whittaker's.' Of course her father was distraught. He must have just found out about the takeover when he'd texted her this morning. 'But he's not going to hurt either one of us.'

'Don't be so sure,' Katie whispered, her eye darts and head swivels becoming increasingly frantic. 'Please, you have to go. Don't let him catch you here. He smashed up the living room already. You have to run away and hide until he calms down. I can stall him. He hardly knows I exist. He won't hurt me. But you...'

'Megan, get in here now!'

Katie shuddered as their father's voice boomed down the hallway.

Weariness and regret added to the guilt tying Megan's stomach into tight greasy knots. But as she went to step into the hallway to face her fate, and the dressing-down she no doubt deserved, Katie grabbed her arm. 'Don't go, Meg. For God's sake, what's wrong with you? He's nuts.'

'He's not nuts,' she said, although he did sound a bit deranged. But losing a company that had been your father's, and his father's before him, could probably do that to any man. 'And he's not going to hurt me.' Their father had always been distant, preoccupied with the company and his commitment to making Whittaker's a success, but he had never raised a hand to either one of them.

She dislodged Katie's fingers from her arm and walked down the hallway to the living room. The first shock came when she walked into the room. For once, Katie hadn't exaggerated. The room Lydia Brady always kept so spotless looked as if a hurricane had hit it. The photos of her and Katie growing up that she'd framed and hung on the walls had been smashed. A table had been upended, leaving fresh flowers crushed and water splattered over the broken glass, but it was the wanton destruction of one of Katie's artworks—the beautiful painting was lying in tattered pieces across the floor—that shocked Megan to the core.

Her father stood by the window, with his back to her. She had expected him to look bowed, to look devastated, had been willing to apologise profusely and then try her best to soothe and persuade and maybe even come up with some kind of solution, if he would let her. But when he turned, his fists clenched at his sides, his usually perfect appearance horribly dishevelled, he didn't look sad, or angry, he looked wild; the whites of his eyes were bloodshot.

'About time the little slut got home.' He strode across the room, the broken picture frames cracking beneath his shoes.

Megan stepped back, the pain in her temples screaming now. He leant past her and slammed the living-room door shut on Katie, who was hovering outside the room. Then propped a chair against the door knob.

'Daddy?' Megan said, the first darts of fear combining with the guilt sitting like a lump of lead in her stomach.

The blow came from nowhere, cracking in the air like a missile shot. She reeled backwards, the pain excruciating as it exploded in her cheekbone.

'You stupid bitch! I'm not your daddy. I kept you two around because I had to—'

She scrambled onto her hands and knees, ignoring the pain in her jaw, the prickle of glass in her palms. He stood over her and hit her again, his fist knocking her shoulder and forcing her down. His foot glanced off her hip then caught the hem of her gown, the blue satin now spattered with blood. Was that her blood?

The metallic taste permeated her mouth.

She couldn't move, the gown twisted around her legs. She could hear her sister's cries, the pounding of her fists against the blocked door.

'Megan? Megan? Answer me, are you okay?'

She tried to shout back, but no sound would come out, the scream locked in her throat as she rolled and saw her father, standing over her, yanking the belt out of the loops on his trousers. He flexed it, snapped it against his palm, as if testing it.

'It was a condition of the damn trust fund your slut of a mother left you.' He was talking, his voice tight with bitterness, but so calm, almost conversational, unlike the wild light in his eyes.

Katie was right. He had gone mad.

'I'm calling the police.' Katie's muffled shouts came through the door. 'Hang on, Megan. I'll get help.'

She heard Katie's running footsteps retreat into silence.

Run, Katie, run. Don't come back.

Her mind screamed as her father ripped away the wrap she had clutched in one hand, then wheeled his arm back. She rolled onto her front, so as not to take the blow on her face.

Pain sliced across her back, the leather biting into her shoulder. She raised her hands, trying to protect her head and the belt cut into the skin of her arm.

'Please, stop.' The plea burst free of the blockage in her throat.

'You deserve this, Lexy,' he screamed her mother's name. 'You did this to me.'

Megan curled into a ball, trying to escape the barrage

of blows. His grunts of exertion, the brutal slap of leather against skin, the scent of lemon polish and blood swirled around her, retreating into darkness, nothingness.

Dario's face appeared, the memory sultry and vivid.

What do you do to me?

The jagged pain in her heart was the last thing to fade as she fell down, down—away from the agony, and the shouts of her mother's name over and over again—into a safe place where no one could find her. Unless she wanted them to.

CHAPTER SIX

'COULD YOU INFORM Miss Megan Whittaker I'm here to see her?' Dario announced to the officious-looking building receptionist.

He didn't like the way Megan had run out on him. He needed to speak with her again. She hadn't done any of the things he had expected of her. He'd been prepared for temper, recriminations, even a guilt trip for deliberately misleading her. He had been ready for all those things and had had all the arguments on hand to explain to her, sensibly and dispassionately, why she was wrong to have read too much into their liaison.

But she hadn't done any of those things. And he couldn't get the picture of her, looking devastated and furious, not with him, but with herself, out of his head. It was foolish of him to feel guilty. He really had nothing to feel bad about. But still he couldn't shake the feeling that he owed her at least a visit.

The memory of her sobs of fulfilment, her sighs of pleasure, her body so sweet and trusting nestled in his arms all through the night, couldn't quite allow him to leave it the way it had ended.

He didn't have to explain himself. They were adults, consenting adults, and everything they'd done together during the night had been mutually pleasurable. But still he felt responsible.

'I'm sorry, sir, there's no answer from the apartment.' The receptionist frowned, the officiousness dropping away to reveal concern. 'Which is odd, because I saw Miss Whittaker go up there ten minutes ago and I know Mr Whittaker and Katie are there, too.'

'Try it again,' he said, the back of his neck prickling.

Something wasn't right. The lift pinged and out of it flew a girl dressed in skinny jeans and a scanty top that left her belly bare. 'De Rossi!' she yelled, racing down the steps leading to the lift and coming to a shuddering halt in front of him. 'You have to rescue her! He's going to kill her, and it's all your fault!'

She grabbed a fistful of his sweater, the fear in her eyes, deep green eyes so like Megan's, searing him to his soul.

'Who are you?' he demanded as he marched towards the lift. But he had already guessed. The prickles became a swarm.

'What's wrong, Katie?' the receptionist shouted out, jettisoning the formality as she confirmed that the frantic girl was Megan's younger sister.

Dario broke into a run, stabbing the lift button ahead of the girl, who shouted to the receptionist, 'Call the police, Marcie. And an ambulance.'

'Which floor?' Dario demanded as they entered the lift together. Cold hard dread gripped his insides—as the memory of another time, another place, assaulted his senses.

Megan's sister punched the button herself. And kept stabbing it as the doors closed, tears streaking down her face now.

'Hurry up, hurry up,' she said in a broken mantra.

'Stop it.' He gripped her shoulders as the lift travelled

up to the tenth floor, her fear forcing him to push the flood of memory and his own terror back.

She collapsed against him, her whole body shaking, and wrapped her arms around his waist. Burying her head against his chest. 'Thank God, you're here. I couldn't get the phone to work in the apartment.'

He rested his palms on her thin shoulders, drew her away, her blind faith in him almost as disturbing as his own irrational fear. 'When we get there, you need to show me where they are.'

'He's locked the door. I couldn't get in.'

The lift finally arrived at the floor. She charged out ahead of him, leading the way to an open apartment door. He heard the sounds first, the rhythmic thuds. He raced down the hallway, kicking open the door the girl indicated at the end with all his might.

The wood shattered and the door flew inward. The explosion of sound startled the man inside, his fist raised, a belt wrapped around it.

Whittaker.

But then Dario saw the woman curled in a foetal position at Lloyd Whittaker's feet. And his mind stalled, the horror gripping his torso so huge and all-consuming he couldn't breathe, couldn't hear anything but the terrified screams in his own head.

'Wake up, Mummy. Please wake up, Mummy.'

'Megan!' The scream from behind him shocked him out of his inertia. The fear was replaced by a feral rage that obliterated everything it its path. Until he couldn't see Lloyd Whittaker any more, or the young woman he'd held in his arms all through the night. All he could see was the man he had fought so many times in his nightmares.

His fist connected with Whittaker's jaw and pain ricocheted up his arm. Whittaker flew backwards and crumpled into a heap, the one punch sending him sprawling into an already broken table, which shattered beneath his weight.

Dario wanted to follow him down, to keep on pounding until the man's face was nothing more than a bloody pulp, but the small mewling cry, like a wild animal caught in a trap, stopped the rage in its tracks.

He watched Katie crouch beside her sister. Megan's beautiful gown, the one he'd eased off her body last night, was torn, the red welts of Whittaker's belt scoring the delicate skin of her shoulders and back.

'She's hurt.' Katie's cries pierced the fog in his brain, dulling the choking fear, the incandescent rage. 'He hurt her. I hate him.'

The fury finally dissolved into a mist—the surge of adrenaline retreating to leave Dario feeling hollow and shaky. He knelt on Megan's other side and gathered her into his arms, determined to concentrate on the task at hand.

They had to get Megan downstairs, to an ambulance. She needed medical care.

Her fragile body curled into his chest as trusting as a child, the bodice of her dress drooping to reveal the dark blue lace that had captivated him the night before.

Ave, o Maria...

He prayed to the virgin mother, the prayer that had been drilled into him as a child by his own mother as he carried Megan's unresisting body through the wreckage of the apartment.

This is not your fault. You are not responsible for the behaviour of a madman.

He kept repeating the words in his mind, his throat dry, his knuckles raw, his arms trembling as he used every ounce of his strength to keep the dark thoughts under control.

As he held her in the lift—Katie stroking her hair and begging her to be okay—Megan shifted in his arms.

He thanked God and all the saints.

'*Cara*, can you hear me?' he asked, gently.

Her eyelids fluttered open, the vicious mark reddening on her cheek making the rage and pain gallop back into his throat.

'*Stai bene, piccola?*' he said, and willed her to be all right.

Please let her be okay.

'*Grazie.*' Her bruised lips tipped into a shy smile—guileless and innocent. She winced, as her eyes closed again.

And the crippling guilt he had been holding so carefully at bay stabbed him right through the heart.

CHAPTER SEVEN

'WE'VE PUT HER into an induced coma, Mr De Rossi. The CT scan was inconclusive and we want to be certain there is no swelling on the brain from the head injury she sustained during the assault.'

Head injury?

The doctor's words whipped at Dario's conscience.

He hated hospitals—the chemical aroma of cleaning fluids and air freshener almost as disturbing as the feeling of powerlessness. He'd been waiting for nearly twenty minutes to see the doctor, his self-control on a knife-edge for a great deal longer—ever since the paramedics had whisked Megan away from him in the foyer three days ago.

After watching Whittaker being treated by paramedics and then taken away in handcuffs, he'd spent hours dealing with his team of lawyers and the police to ensure any assault charges against him would be dropped. He'd then spent further hours being questioned as a witness to Whittaker's assault on his daughter. And after that he had been forced to give a press conference, the media swarming around the hint of a juicy story like flies on a rotting carcass. There had already been a barrage of reports on the Internet, and photographs of him and Megan dancing at the Westchester and their subsequent departure. All of which had fuelled speculation about how Megan had ended up being rushed to hospital the next morning, and how her father had ended up in handcuffs.

As soon as the press conference was over, Dario's first instinct had been to rush to Megan's bedside at the exclusive private hospital in Murray Hill where he'd insisted she be transferred to avoid the press hordes. But he'd forced himself not to give in to that knee-jerk reaction.

Going to see Megan in the hospital would only increase the press speculation about them, he'd reasoned. He and Megan were not a couple, they were never meant to be anything more than a one-night stand—and, despite the horror of her father's attack and his own cursory involvement in it, he was not responsible for her.

But after he had been waiting three torturous days for news of Megan's recovery, Dario's ability to be patient and circumspect about the situation was at an end.

He wanted to know what the hell was going on, because the reports he'd been getting had been inconclusive, contradictory and wholly unsatisfactory. She should be awake and lucid by now, surely?

Unfortunately, the decision to go to the hospital and see for himself how she was had not helped calm his temper in the slightest—because he'd been thwarted by a brick wall of white coats and medical jargon as soon as he'd arrived and now the good Dr Hernandez, all five feet nothing of her, was the last straw.

'I wish to see her,' he reiterated.

The truth was, he *had* to see her, to be sure she was okay. The faraway look in her eyes, that bruised cheek and bloodied lip, the welts left by her father's belt on her shoulder blades had been tormenting him for days. He needed to touch her, feel her skin warm beneath his fingers, before he would be able to breathe again.

'Her sister is her only authorised visitor, Mr De Rossi.'

'Is Katie with her now?' he asked.

'No, I insisted she went home to rest.'

'Then Megan's alone?' He didn't want her to be alone. What if she woke and no one was there? Wouldn't she be scared after everything she'd been through?

'Miss Whittaker is still unconscious and will remain so, until we're ready to bring her out of the induced coma later today.' The doctor continued dispassionately, 'But when that happens I am only going to authorise close family to visit her.'

And of course she had no other family than Katie, and her bastard of a father. Every protective instinct Dario possessed, instincts he'd never even realised he had, rose up inside him. They had been as close as any two people could get four nights ago, but he could see that wasn't going to wash with Dr Hernandez.

'I am paying for her treatment. I insist on seeing her.'

Maybe it was irrational, the fear that had gripped him ever since he'd stormed into her apartment building to find her being brutalised by her father, but he couldn't wait to see her any longer.

Dr Hernandez drew herself up to her full height, which did not reach his chin, and levelled a sanguine look at him. She didn't look intimidated in the slightest.

'This isn't about what *you* want, Mr De Rossi. It's about what's best for my patient.'

'And leaving her alone is best for her?' he demanded, his frustration increasing. This woman hadn't seen her curled on the floor like a terrified child.

'That doesn't alter the fact that you're not related to her, Mr De Rossi, and I can't authorise a—'

'We're engaged,' he said, grasping at the only connection he could think of to give him the access he needed. 'And I'm not leaving until I see her. Does that alter things?'

The doctor's features softened and she gave a weary sigh. 'Okay, Mr De Rossi, you can see her when she wakes up. But that could be a while.'

'I'll wait.'

She tucked her hands into the pockets of her white coat, the sympathetic look annoying him more. 'Why don't you go home first and get some rest? You look exhausted.'

Of course he was exhausted; he hadn't slept for three damn days. 'I'm not leaving.'

'It could be several hours before your fiancée wakes up.'

The quaint, romantic term gave him a jolt, but he ignored it. Seeing Megan was the only way to make the anxiety that had been lodged in the pit of his stomach ever since the attack go away. 'And I intend to be here when that happens.' On that point, he refused to budge.

If he returned to his penthouse, the memories of that night would be waiting for him. Memories he couldn't seem to shake. The sweet sighs of her release, the hours spent touching and tempting her. And worse still, if he closed his eyes, the nightmares would chase him. He would see her bruised and battered body, feel her dead weight in his arms as he carried her into the lift, trying not to hurt her more.

'Then sit down before you fall down,' the doctor said, not unkindly, indicating one of the waiting area's leather armchairs. The pity in the woman's warm brown eyes added discomfort to his frustration—and the dazed feeling that had started to descend without warning.

'I'm not going to fall down,' he said, locking his knees, just to be sure.

'Good, because I have no intention of catching you,' the doctor returned. Gripping his elbow, she led him to the armchair she had indicated. 'What Miss Whittaker needs now most of all is rest,' she added, her voice floating somewhere over his head and not quite coming into complete focus any more. 'She's suffered a terrible trauma.'

'I understand that,' he said, his knees giving way as the adrenaline that had been charging through his veins for days finally deserted him. 'Which is why I intend to stay.'

'I suppose it can't do any harm to have her loved ones close by.'

Her loved ones?

The doctor's softly spoken words made no sense.

But as she left the room Dario sank his head into his hands. He raked his fingers through his hair and gripped his head to stop it dropping off his shoulders. He didn't have time to worry about the doctor's misconceptions. He'd said what he had to say to give him the access he needed.

He had to make sure Megan was okay. And that Whittaker paid for his crimes. Then he would be able to forget about the attack—and get a decent night's sleep again.

His smartphone buzzed and he fished it out of his pocket. He scrolled through the list of missed calls and texts. His gaze snagged on Jared Caine's text.

Saw the news. Nice work knocking that creep unconscious, buddy. Here if you need me.

The simple, succinct message made his chest tighten—which had to be the exhaustion.

He and Jared were friends. They went way back. Ten years back to be exact, to a dark rainy night in the West Village—when Dario had been a twenty-year-old Italian upstart with a fledgling investment corporation making a name for itself on Wall Street and Jared had been a fifteen-year-old street punk who'd made the mistake of trying to pick another former street punk's pocket.

Dario had taken Jared under his wing after that night because the boy's cynicism and street smarts, his thirst for something better in life and his too-old eyes, had reminded Dario of himself.

But somewhere in the last decade, as Jared had forged his own path, shearing off all but a few of his rough edges, to become a smart, erudite and ambitious security advisor with a growing portfolio, Dario had come to rely on the younger man's friendship and loyalty.

And right now he could use Jared's professional help, because his buddy owned and operated one of the best, and certainly the hungriest, private security and investigative firms in the city.

Dario keyed in a quick text, requesting a meeting soon to discuss Whittaker's case. Not that Dario didn't trust New York's Finest, but the NYPD didn't have the resources of De Rossi Corp. Dario wanted Megan's father prosecuted to the full extent of the law.

He had seen the look in Whittaker's eyes when he'd punched him. He knew exactly what that wild glassy sheen indicated. And if the fifty-something CEO had a substance-abuse problem he had managed to keep secret, there would no doubt be other stuff they could use to crucify him.

Jared's reply came back.

I'll get working on it. Then we can arrange a meet at my place. More private.

The tightness in Dario's chest eased.

He laid his head back against the armchair, his galloping pulse slowing to a canter, but blinked to keep the foggy feeling at bay.

No sleep yet, not until he'd seen Megan. And assured himself once and for all she was okay.

Because only then would he be able to get the picture of her cowering at Whittaker's feet, beaten and brutalised, out of his head.

CHAPTER EIGHT

S<small>HE COULD HEAR VOICES.</small>

The first was her sister's.

'Meggy, please come back, you have to wake up now.' She could hear the panic and fear in Katie's voice. But she didn't want to come back just yet. Couldn't she stay here?

But then she heard another voice, much lower and more assured, which didn't plead, it insisted.

'Open your eyes for me, *cara.*'

She frowned. She wanted to be a little bit annoyed. Why did she have to come back? Staying where she was felt so much easier. But that voice, it was so compelling. It made her feel important. Significant. Special. It sounded so sure. And so safe. And so deliciously seductive.

The tingling sensation in her fingers became something more. A ripple of sensation. Warmth spread over her hand and her eyelids fluttered open.

Dario?

Heat flushed through her at the memory of that seductive mouth on hers. But why did he look so different from the last time she'd seen him, in his penthouse apartment, after they'd made love?

His hair had been dishevelled then too, but it looked a mess now. His jaw was covered in dark stubble and his eyes... He hadn't had those bruised smudges under his eyes, had he?

'*Ciao*, Megan. *Come va?*' The lyrical Italian washed over her. But then his sensual lips tipped up at the edges as he translated. 'How are you feeling?'

That smile, she remembered that smile. So sexy. Heat settled in her abdomen and she tried to speak. But all that came out was a husky croak.

He held her hand and pressed it to his lips. The prickle of stubble against her knuckles made her aware of a few other aches and pains. A lot of other aches and pains. Where had they come from? She remembered being sore after their lovemaking, but not this sore.

'Water?' he asked.

She nodded.

Cradling her head, he held a cup to her lips, directing the straw into her mouth. She took a sip, the cool water easing the rawness in her throat. Why was she so thirsty?

'Okay?' he said.

'Yes,' she said, despite all those unexplained aches and pains. 'Where are we? Is this your bedroom?' Had he taken her upstairs? She was sure he had. She could remember the slow glide of his fingers over sensitive flesh, the prickling spray of the water in his power shower, the scent of sandalwood soap that had clung to his skin and hers later, much later, as they lay together on Egyptian cotton sheets. But everything else felt so disjointed. And this didn't feel like his bedroom, the cloying scent of roses and the persistent sound of something beeping confusing her.

'You're in hospital,' he said, placing the cup back on a bedside table.

'I am? Why?' That didn't sound right. What was she doing in a hospital? 'Did I have an accident?'

'You don't remember?' he asked.

'No, I... I remember being with you and...' The heat suffused her skin. Should she tell him? But he looked concerned. She didn't want him to worry. She didn't want him to think for even a second that she hadn't enjoyed herself. It had been a little sore at first. Just as she had suspected, he wasn't a small man...anywhere. But it had been glorious after that. She wanted him to know that. She thought she'd told him this already, but maybe she'd only thought it.

'I remember it was wonderful. You were wonderful. But that's all I can remember.' Had she made a complete muppet of herself? Fallen over in his power shower? Tripped down the stairs leading up to the mezzanine? That would be just like her, to knock herself unconscious after the best sex of her life. The only proper sex of her life.

'What accident did I have?' she asked, when he simply stared at her, his gaze searching her face as if he was looking for something. Something important.

'Meg, you're awake.' Katie's excited voice pierced her aching head before her sister bounced into view beside Dario.

He started to move aside to make room for Katie, who looked overjoyed to see her. But as he went to let go of her hand, Megan's grip tightened.

'No, don't. Don't go.'

She didn't want to let go of him, not yet. She liked having him there. Something dark and scary seemed to be lurking just out of reach, and she didn't want to let it come any closer. With Dario there, holding her hand, she knew it wouldn't be able to. He was such a force of nature. He would never let it hurt her, whatever it was. And he cared about her. She knew he did. Because she could hear his voice in her memory telling her everything would be okay.

He squeezed her hand back. 'What is it, *cara*?'

'Could you stay with me?'

He hesitated for a moment, but then he sat back down, still holding her hand. 'If you want.'

She could see Katie swivelling her head between the two of them, her eyes widening. But she didn't have the energy to care. She had known she would have to tell Katie about Dario, and everything that had happened last night at the Westchester Ball, because it was impossible to keep anything secret from her sister. But she was more than happy to let Katie draw her own conclusions now, because she wasn't exactly sure herself what had happened any more. Except that it had been glorious. And just having Dario look at her like that, as if he would keep her safe no matter what, was enough to make the aches and pains from her mysterious accident fade away.

Along with the dark, scary thing lurking in the shadows.

A short, rotund, middle-aged Hispanic woman with a friendly face and gentle hands appeared and introduced herself as Dr Hernandez.

She checked Megan's pulse, shone a light into her eyes and then spoke to her in a soft, even voice.

She asked Megan all sorts of silly questions, like her age and her name, and Katie's name and their relationship. And where they lived. And what year it was. The doctor asked her about Dario and if she remembered him. Of course she did, she said, as the blush spread up her chest.

Thank goodness the lighting was muted in here. Or this interrogation could become really awkward, especially with Katie sitting there listening to every word.

But then the questions became more confusing.

'Do you remember your relationship to Mr De Rossi?'

She felt Dario's hand clench hers, his jaw stiffening.

'I...' She wasn't sure how to answer that. She didn't want to seem even more gauche, or clueless, than she did already, but at the same time he was here, holding her hand, so maybe he wouldn't mind her mentioning it. 'We're lovers,' she said, deciding that sounded a little less embarrassing than *We shared a night of the hottest sex I've ever had.*

'Do you remember that you're engaged to Mr De Rossi?'

Huh?

'What? Seriously?' Katie said, echoing Megan's confused thoughts. 'You're kidding?'

Her little sister crowded in on her and Dario and the doctor again.

Really? They were engaged? That was, well, surprising. Astonishing even. She couldn't remember the exact details, but hadn't they only met last night?

Dario's grip stayed firm, though, and he didn't jump in to deny it. The look on his face was guarded somehow but intense.

Even though she couldn't remember falling in love with Dario—which was probably a bad thing—being engaged to him, having him fall in love with her, felt like a good thing. Or at least not a bad thing. It made her feel protected, coveted, the way she hadn't felt since she was a little girl and her mother— She cut off that thought.

No, she wasn't going to think about her mother. Because it would take away the happy, floaty buzz, the giddy excitement in her chest that thinking about Dario gave her.

And being with him. Now. For ever. That felt pretty good too. Because as well as him being there to protect her, he could give her lots more of the hot, sexy times that she *could* remember from their night together—their apparently very eventful night together.

Really, it was all good. Except the not remembering part. But that would come back in time. Surely no woman would forget falling in love with Dario De Rossi for long?

'I...' She paused. She didn't want to lie to Dario, but she

didn't want to hurt his feelings either. And if they were engaged, she must have agreed to it. 'I think I remember it.'

'Do you remember anything about your father? About what happened?' the doctor said.

Thoughts butted into her head. Not happy, or floaty thoughts, this time, but sharp, discordant, jarring ones. Panic tore at her raw throat, and she began to shake.

The beeping in her ears got louder, more persistent.

'I don't...' She couldn't speak past the blockage in her throat, that dark, scary figure lurking nearby, encroaching on her peripheral vision. 'I don't want to think about that.'

She didn't know why, but she knew thinking about her father would be bad.

'Shh, Megan.' Dario leant over her, still holding her hand; he stroked her hair back from her forehead, the intense look pulling her away from the fear. 'It's okay. Look at me, *cara.*' He caught her chin in firm fingers, making her concentrate on him, that turbulent blue gaze forcing the fear back. 'You're okay. Do you understand?'

The words echoed in her heart, folding around her like a soft blanket, keeping her safe.

'Yes, but don't go.' She wanted to go back to sleep, but she couldn't stop shaking, the terror still too close.

'I won't,' he said, his voice so determined she knew he meant it. *'Te lo prometto.'*

I promise you.

'Relax, Megan,' the doctor said. 'I'm going to give you something to help with that.' A warm tingling feeling seeped into her vein, spreading up her arm and enveloping her in a beautiful fog. She floated on it, sinking into the cloud, soothed by the pressure of Dario's hand and his deep compelling voice telling her again that everything would be okay.

She held on to his hand, knowing it was true, as long as she didn't let him go.

* * *

'What just happened in there?' Dario could feel his frustration levels rising as he stalked after Dr Hernandez. He and Katie had been double teaming for ten hours, waiting for Megan to come out of her coma. And now this. 'How can she remember nothing of the attack?' he demanded as the doctor stopped at the nurses' station.

He shoved his fists into the pockets of his trousers, the fear on Megan's face still haunting him. How had this happened? He didn't feel less responsible now, he felt more so.

'Your fiancée has suffered a serious emotional and physical trauma, Mr De Rossi,' the doctor said with complete equanimity as she jotted something down on Megan's chart. 'It's quite possible she has blanked some of the events from that day.' The woman's clear brown gaze focused on his face. 'The good news is, she remembers you and your engagement. Your presence calmed her down considerably, which will be useful in the weeks and months ahead as she recovers.'

Months. He couldn't be responsible for her for months. He wasn't even her real fiancé. He knew he should point this out to Hernandez, but the memory of Megan clutching his hand and looking at him with such faith in her eyes made the words clog in his throat. He could not deny the connection now.

Until Megan was well again, and she had her memory back—*all* her memories back—she would be defenceless.

'I can't believe you proposed after one night!' Katie appeared at his elbow. 'That must have been some night.' The girl's scepticism was, of course, entirely justified, but the astonished look spiked his annoyance.

'Your sister is a remarkable woman,' he heard himself say.

'I know she is,' the girl said. 'But I'm surprised you do.'

He could hear the bite of cynicism in her tone. And it occurred to him that, although Katie was the younger sister, she had none of Megan's faith in the inherent goodness of people.

'He certainly never did,' she added.

'I am not your father,' he said, the comparison annoying him more. 'I appreciate your sister.'

'I get that, or I guess you wouldn't have asked her to marry you,' she said, not sounding convinced. 'But you still don't strike me as the sort of guy to fall hopelessly in love in the space of one night.'

She was certainly correct about that.

'Who said anything about love?' he asked, his temper kicking up another notch. He didn't need the fifth degree from a teenager. 'Megan and I are well matched. And she understands this engagement is one of convenience.' Or she would, as soon as she regained her memory and he could break it off.

But until then he would have to maintain this fiction. He could not leave Megan so vulnerable.

There was the police investigation to consider, the subsequent trial and, on top of all that, the press, who had been camped outside the hospital for days. How could he leave the young woman who had gripped his hand with such fear in her eyes to fend off all that alone?

Maybe he had not wanted the job, but who else was there? A nineteen-year-old art student was the only other candidate.

'I don't believe you.' Katie interrupted his thoughts. 'Underneath all her pragmatism and business savvy, Megan's a romantic. If she agreed to marry you, she must think she's in love with you.'

'She needs someone to protect her. I have the money and resources to do that until she is well. She understands that.'

Megan had struck him from the first as a pragmatic young woman, astute and intelligent. Maybe she had a blind spot where her father was concerned, but however fragile her mental state she must have made a choice to agree with Dario's deception in there. A subconscious choice maybe, but a choice nonetheless. However faulty her memory, she could hardly have remembered a proposal that did not occur.

He flexed his fingers, recalling the feel of her hand, so small, clasping his, as she begged him not to leave her. And another memory swirled in his consciousness, making his lungs squeeze in his chest.

Please save me, Dario.

He took a steadying breath, forcing himself to shake off the debilitating images from his past.

He had to concentrate on the present. The way forward was simple. He could not abandon Megan until she was well. But their situation had nothing to do with love. He and Megan understood that, even if Megan's sister did not.

'I'm sorry. I don't know why I'm having a go at you,' Katie said, as the fluorescent lighting caught the bluish smudges under her eyes. The girl was exhausted. She'd been keeping this vigil a great deal longer than he had, he realised. She dragged her hand through her hair. 'I'm the one who let her walk into that room.'

'It is pointless to blame yourself.' He gave the girl an awkward pat on the shoulder. Then shoved his hand back into his pocket.

Consoling distraught teenagers was as far out of his comfort zone as pretending to be someone's fiancé.

'You should go home, get some sleep,' he said. 'I will stay and ascertain what is to be done next and contact you in the morning.'

Katie looked at him, then back at the door to Megan's

room, clearly torn. He was struck by the closeness of the bond between the two sisters, despite their personality differences. He would do well to remember that.

'There is little more either one of us can do now,' he added. He might not want this responsibility, but he was not about to shirk it—until he had come up with a coherent plan for Megan's recovery.

'Okay, I guess she trusts you,' she said. 'And you did save her life.'

The words should have made him feel more burdened, but, oddly, instead he felt strangely relieved as he watched Megan's sister leave. As long as he had complete control of the situation, he would be in a position to resolve it, to everyone's satisfaction.

'Dr Hernandez…' He turned to the doctor, who had been scribbling on Megan's chart while he and Katie talked. 'Can you tell me when Megan's memory will return?' The first order of business was to discover the depths of the problem.

'I'm afraid not. Medicine is not an exact science, Mr De Rossi. We'll run some more tests, have her speak to a psychiatrist to ascertain as much as we can about the amnesia. If there is no neurological cause, though, I would expect Megan to remember the events in more detail once she is emotionally strong enough to deal with them.'

'Get her whatever she needs. Money is no object,' he said, prepared to pay whatever it took.

'Either way, she should be ready to leave the hospital in a week or so,' the doctor continued. 'Her physical injuries are healing well. And she'll be able to get the rest and recuperation she needs much better in a home environment.'

He swore under his breath. The doctor was right, of course, but what home environment did she have? She could not return to her old apartment, which had been repossessed as soon as Whittaker had been arrested and the state of his finances revealed. And anyway, it was the site of the attack. Katie was now staying with the girls' old housekeeper in Brooklyn, having refused his offer of financial aid. But Megan couldn't stay there—it was too small and would not protect her from press attention. He and Katie had been running the gauntlet of photographers and reporters while taking it in turns to visit the hospital. Megan would need somewhere far away from the media spotlight.

'By the way, Mr De Rossi,' the doctor cut into his thoughts as she finished writing on Megan's chart and handed it back to the nurse. 'You mentioned the possibility of Megan being pregnant. We ran the test as requested and it came back negative.'

Thank goodness.

Dario's lungs released, the relief making him light-headed. He'd requested the test a few hours before, his mind finally functioning well enough to realise that Megan might not have had time to take the necessary precautions before her father attacked her. Maybe she hadn't even needed the emergency contraception. Either way, this at least was good news.

But before he could suck in another calming breath the doctor added, 'Of course, there's always a slight chance of a false negative this soon after possible conception, but it's unlikely.'

A false negative? What on earth did that even mean?

CHAPTER NINE

'Hey, man, wasn't expecting you tonight.' Jared yawned, then squinted at Dario out of sleep-deprived eyes.

Dario glanced at his watch. And winced. Two a.m. 'Sorry, I did not realise the time.'

'No problem. Come on in.' His friend wearing only a pair of sweat pants pushed open the heavy metal door to his loft apartment. 'Want a beer? You look like you could use one,' Jared added, padding into the apartment ahead of Dario.

He probably shouldn't have come over at this hour. But for the first time in his life, he needed help and complete confidentiality, and Jared was the only person he trusted that much.

The guy was the closest thing Dario had to family. Or what Dario figured a brother would be like. Someone who would help you out in a jam, no questions asked, but didn't pry into your private life. And that was what he needed right now. Because he'd been roaming Murray Hill like a zombie for a couple of hours, ever since he'd left Megan at the hospital, trying to figure out a workable solution.

'You look terrible,' Jared said as he cracked open a beer and handed it to Dario.

'It's been a long four days.' Dario took the beer and

chugged a mouthful of the yeasty lager. Had it really been only four days since he'd had Megan in his arms? Soft and sweet and sobbing for release?

Stop right there, amico.

He took another long pull of lager, struggling to ignore the inevitable swell of heat.

He needed to stop torturing himself with thoughts of that night, because he wasn't going to have Megan in his arms again. The only way to square the subterfuge with his conscience was if he didn't sleep with her. She was fragile, emotionally as well as physically, so until she was fully recovered he couldn't even consider making love to her. He swallowed. Sleeping with her *again*, he corrected.

And not even then.

She was trusting and innocent and this situation had become far too complex already. He preferred women who knew the score, so that he could keep his sex life simple and his affairs shallow and short-lived. Megan had got under his skin to an extent that no other woman ever had, and circumstances had done the rest. All of which made him supremely uncomfortable.

'Yeah, I gathered that from the press reports on late-night TV.' Jared took a swig of his own beer and leaned against the counter top, the searching look only winding the knot in Dario's gut tighter. 'How's the new fiancée doing?'

The beer hit Dario's tonsils and he jerked forward in mid-sip.

Jared gave him a hearty thump on the back.

'The press got hold of that already?' Dario managed at last, his voice a hoarse whisper. Someone at the hospital must have leaked the information—which was all the more reason to get Megan out of there, out of the city, as soon as she was well enough to travel.

'So it's true?' Jared said dispassionately, but the relaxed pose was history. 'You guys are engaged?'

'Yes,' Dario said, his tired brain starting to knot along with his gut. He needed to get some sleep. He'd been running on adrenaline for hours; it was dulling his thought processes.

'You want to tell me how that happened?' Jared said.

'It's complicated,' Dario said.

'I gathered that.' Jared picked his beer back up off the counter, and used it to point at the long leather couches that made up the apartment's seating area. 'Let's take a load off.' He led the way across the large open-plan living space. Dario followed.

Jared settled on one of the luxury couches. The leather creaked as he propped his bare feet on the coffee table. And waited for Dario to speak. The younger man's pragmatic presence helped to settle the nerves dancing in Dario's stomach as he stared out at the night time NoHo cityscape visible through the wall of glass that had replaced the old loft's loading bay doors. But the compulsion to explain the situation to Jared still surprised him.

He never talked about his personal life to anyone. He'd been a self-contained unit since he was eight years old. Had forced himself to be. Leaning on other people, relying on them, just made you weak. But his personal life hadn't been this complicated ever. And he hadn't been blindsided like this, by events beyond his control, since he was that eight-year-old boy. And he didn't like it, because that was a feeling he'd promised himself he'd never have again.

'Megan doesn't remember what happened with her father,' he said, fixing his gaze on the blinking light of a plane above the dark shapes of the city's skyline. 'They ran some tests, got the opinion of the top psychologist in NYC and a head trauma specialist from Baltimore who's supposed to be the best in her field.' He'd had the woman flown in especially, to give a second opinion. 'They don't think the memory loss is to do with her head injury, which was minor.' The relief he felt at that piece of information was still palpable. 'More likely it's to do with the emotional trauma. A form of PTSD. A man Megan loved and trusted turned on her like an animal, so she's blacked it out.'

He drew his thumbnail through the label on the beer bottle, watched it tear into jagged pieces.

There was only one thing to do. It didn't matter if it would complicate his life for a while. Seeing Megan's anguish when Hernandez had mentioned her father, her vibrant hair rioting around that alabaster face and her deep emerald eyes wild with terror, had pulled at something deep inside him that he could not deny. She'd gripped his fingers as if he were the only solid object in the midst of a hurricane. She needed him and he couldn't simply desert her.

'I see what you mean by complicated,' Jared said.

Dario looked up from his contemplation of the beer bottle, remembering his friend was there.

'She needs rest and as little stress as possible, according to the doctors,' he said. 'The press furore is only going to get more insane when Whittaker is charged. I think it is best if I take her out of the country. If she is my fiancée I am in a position to make those arrangements, to keep her safe and protected until she recovers.'

Jared sent him a level stare. 'If? So this isn't a real engagement. Does she know that?'

'Maybe, maybe not. But she has accepted it without question, so it hardly matters,' Dario said. Maybe it was complicated and confused, but it all made perfect sense if you looked at it rationally.

Megan was in no position to make these decisions for

herself. And even if she hadn't been assaulted, Dario didn't trust her to make sensible decisions about her own safety. She was far too trusting at the best of times, and these were not the best of times.

'Okay.' Jared leant forward, resting his elbows on his knees—accepting Dario's reasoning.

But then, he hadn't expected Jared to question him.

His friend was even more cynical about relationships than he was. To the best of Dario's knowledge, Jared had never kept a lover for more than one night. Manhattan high society was strewn with the bruised hearts of women Jared had cast off before they could mean anything to him. He suspected that emotional isolation had something to do with Jared's childhood, or rather the lack of it, but he'd never asked; any more than he had asked about the cigarette burns on his friend's forearms, which were barely visible now, or the other scars that had faded in the years since he'd offered Jared a bed for the night in his apartment, before referring the homeless boy to the proper authorities. Because Jared's past was none of his business.

'I was going to work up a report for you on the case,' Jared said. 'You want the high points, before we discuss the particulars of how you're going to get your new fiancée out of the country?' Jared asked, the efficient, down-to-earth approach reassuring.

Dario nodded. 'Yeah.'

'Just as you suspected, Megan's father was high as a kite when he attacked her,' Jared began. 'According to my contact in the NYPD he's had a major cocaine habit for years. His girlfriend Annalise Maybury—now his ex-girlfriend—told the detectives as much under questioning. And there's something else, something I found out on my own after doing some digging,' Jared continued, the cynicism in his voice even sharper than usual. 'They're not his daughters.'

'What?'

'Megan and her sister, they're not his biological kids. He's known for years—got them paternity tested without their knowledge when they were children after the mom ran off with one of her lovers. Whittaker only kept them around, pretended he was still their old man, because he was busy mooching off the trust fund their mom left them. Which is all gone now, just in case you were wondering.'

'Bastardo!' Dario's anger curled around his heart, turning from red-hot rage to ice-cold fury.

He'd known Whittaker was a poor excuse for a CEO, and an even worse excuse for a father. But he'd never suspected the cocaine use, or the violence, so adding embezzlement and exploitation to that didn't seem like much of a stretch. But how much more vulnerable did this make Megan?

Megan and her sister had no money. And the press were bound to find out the truth about her parentage and splash it all over the papers and the Internet to feed the public's insatiable hunger for scandal. He'd seen the paparazzi shots of her as a teenager at her mother's funeral. She'd been scared and alone but also fiercely protective of her little sister.

When the press got hold of this story, it would be worse.

The memory of the welts on Megan's shoulder blades leapt out from the recesses of his tired mind, only to blur into a bloodier, more terrifying image. The sickening thuds of fists hitting flesh, the high-pitched sound of his mother's screams and the scent of stale cigarette smoke and cheap chianti assaulted him.

'Hey, man, are you okay?'

Jared's question drew him back to the present.

He blocked the image out, the way he had learned to over the years. But the return of the old nightmare left him shaken. His hand trembled as he took a last swig of his beer. Something he did not need Jared, or anyone else, to see.

'Yes.' He placed the bottle on the table between them. 'Can you give this information to the police?'

'Sure. I'll send them a copy of my report. Anything else you need on this?'

'I need your help to get Megan and her sister, Katie, out of the country without alerting the press as soon as Megan is well enough to travel. And me as well.' His mind was made up. There was no other solution. And with Katie there as a chaperone, he ought to find it easier to keep his mind out of the gutter.

Megan's memory would return soon, he had to believe that, because he intended to do everything in his power to ensure she felt safe and secure and well rested enough for that to happen—which included him being by her side. And when her memory did return, he wanted to be there. Just in case there were other complications.

The possibility of a pregnancy was small, according to Hernandez, after she had dropped her bombshell about a false negative on the test, and he wasn't going to worry about it overmuch. But he also wasn't taking any chances.

'I'd advise against taking the kid sister with you,' Jared said, interrupting Dario's thoughts.

'What? Why?'

'She might need to be available for Whittaker's arraignment,' he said.

'But surely our sworn statements are enough until the case comes to trial?' Dario asked. Witnesses weren't usually called for an arraignment.

'True enough, but I wouldn't risk it. Whittaker might

be low on funds, but he's no fool. He's managed to beg, borrow and steal enough for a top-flight legal team. He's saying you inflicted the wounds on your lover in a jealous rage. Neither the police nor the prosecutor's office are buying that. But if Megan's lost her memory, Katie is the only reliable witness to the actual assault. You can make a good case for taking Megan out of the country to recuperate until the trial, and if you're her fiancé it makes sense for you to go with her. But you spirit Katie out of the country too, just before the guy's arraigned, and I guarantee you Whittaker's defence team will try and use it. The kid sister stays, or you're taking a risk of this case not even getting to trial.'

Dario swore, his head starting to pound. 'Okay, Katie stays. I'll tell her tomorrow. She won't like it.' And neither did he. Being alone with her big sister wasn't going to make resisting Megan any easier. 'We cannot risk having Whittaker weasel out of paying for what he has done. Katie will understand that.' Because he suspected, unlike Megan, Katie had never had any delusions about their father. Or rather, the man who had pretended to be their father. 'Can I ask you another favour in that case?'

'Fire away,' Jared said.

'Can you protect Katie from the press once we're gone?' The girl was brave and bold, but she was also reckless and unpredictable and young.

Jared nodded. 'Consider it done.'

'I should warn you though,' Dario said, recalling his run-in with Katie earlier that day. 'She may not be co-operative. She is not as trusting or as amenable as Megan.'

'I think I can handle a hot-headed kid,' Jared said. 'I happen to be a professional.'

Dario's lips lifted in what felt like his first smile in days at the wry tone. 'Thanks.'

Downing the rest of the beer, Dario got up from the couch and shook Jared's hand. 'I'll speak to Katie tomorrow.' Not a conversation he was looking forward to. 'In the meantime, can you liaise with the police and the prosecutor's office to let them know what's going on? Then work up a plan to get us out of the country undetected.'

'Got it,' Jared said as he walked Dario to the door of the apartment. 'Where are you guys headed?'

'Isadora.'

He'd bought the island off the coast of Sicily five years ago, when the company had made its first billion in turnover. And had finished renovating the five-bedroom villa on it over a year ago. He'd already had a visit scheduled to the island once the Whittaker takeover was finalised, to check up on the many investments he was making in the island's infrastructure. And get some much-needed R and R.

'Nice,' Jared said, before bidding him goodbye.

Dario wasn't so sure. When he was not so tired, he might appreciate the irony that his visit to the island was now likely to be the opposite of relaxing.

CHAPTER TEN

THE HELICOPTER TOUCHED down on a helipad hewn out of volcanic rock. Megan breathed in the scent of sea salt and citrus, her eyes expanding with wonder at the heart-stopping view as the blades whirled to a stop.

A path meandered through terraces of lemon groves to a white sand beach. Dario's villa stood on the clifftop, its elegant stone walls adorned by grapevines and wisteria, the dark wood shutters open to let in the sunny spring morning, which was a good ten degrees hotter than Manhattan.

Dario leaned over her to undo her seat belt. 'You're awake? Are you feeling well?' he asked, solicitous and concerned.

'Yes, I woke up a while ago,' she said. She'd noticed him sitting beside her when she opened her eyes, busy keying in data on his smartphone, apparently uninterested in the staggering view as the helicopter swooped over the Mediterranean and then hugged the coastline of the stunningly picturesque island.

She hadn't wanted to disturb him, so she'd gazed out of the window and absorbed the breathtaking vistas while trying to get her careering pulse and erratic heartbeat under control.

It all seemed like a strange and wonderful dream. So strange and wonderful, she didn't know what to make of it.

Everything had happened so fast. Ever since Dario had told her they were engaged in the hospital three days ago. And yet at the same time, in a sort of delayed motion, each new and astonishing experience leaving her struggling to make sense of them. Frankly, it was all a bit too wonderful. As if she couldn't quite believe it was real.

She had led a privileged life, having attended private schools and lived in well-appointed homes in London and New York. She considered herself to be fairly cosmopolitan, with a smattering of Italian and French, having spent her childhood and adolescence living on two continents.

But nothing could have prepared her for the opulence and luxury of the world Dario lived in.

They'd been whisked from the hospital to JFK in a fleet of limousines in the middle of the night, then transported across the Atlantic on a private jet. The cordon bleu meal served on bone china crockery with sterling silver cutlery, followed by a night—alone—on a king-size bed in the sleek aircraft. The helicopter ride had been yet another new experience—as exhilarating as it was unsettling. But by far the most daunting thing had been having Dario by her side during every waking hour.

He'd been so careful with her, as if she were made of spun glass and might break at any minute. But while his care had made her feel cherished and safe in the hospital, now it was starting to feel stifling. He was such a commanding man, both physically and professionally. And she knew she wasn't yet one hundred per cent, because she still couldn't remember a thing about their engagement, or her accident. She didn't want to seem ungrateful, but she couldn't help wondering how Dario had managed to fall in love with her, when he obviously thought she was a bit pathetic.

She also couldn't quite fathom how she'd agreed to

marry him, when he made the air seize in her chest and her stomach do backflips every time he looked at her with those piercing blue eyes.

How were they going to have any kind of married life together, when his presence by her side made it hard for her to breathe?

Then again, at least she wasn't the only one who found him a bit intimidating.

He never raised his voice, but everyone they came into contact with on their journey—his PA, the drivers, the pilots, even the passport authorities—did his bidding without question. Everyone except his friend Jared, who'd talked to Dario like an equal when he had come to tell Megan he would be keeping an eye on Katie while they were away, on Dario's instructions.

She had wondered why Katie would need anyone keeping an eye on her, and debated warning him that Katie wasn't the easiest person to handle. But, in the end, she'd decided not to say anything. After all, Katie was more than capable of speaking for herself, and it had been so thoughtful of Dario to worry about her sister's welfare.

A car and driver arrived at the heliport as Dario helped her down from the cockpit. His firm fingers on her arm made her pulse jump and jive. She concentrated on the spurt of adrenaline as he left her side to go to talk to the pilot.

Gift horse—mouth? Hello? Stop looking! Why can't you just enjoy the thrill? You're tired and a little overwhelmed, that's all. A staggeringly gorgeous man is in love with you. This is not something to have a panic attack about.

A team of staff members arrived in a fleet of SUVs to unload a series of bags, boxes and trunks from the helicopter's hold. Luggage Megan had never seen before.

'*Cara*, are you ready?' Dario said, returning to lead her to the car.

'Yes, but… I just realised I didn't pack anything for the trip.' She didn't recognise the luggage, so it must be Dario's. 'Do you think I could order some clothes?' There had been some expensive clothes waiting for her on his private jet to change into when she'd arrived from the hospital, which had been wonderful and had made her feel a little teary—her fiancé appeared to think of everything. There had even been a ton of expensive creams, make-up and haircare products for all her toiletry needs, and a designer negligee in the plane's bedroom—although the seductive confection of silk and lace had seemed a little pointless when Dario had worked through the flight on his laptop instead of joining her.

But she couldn't expect the luggage fairy to keep providing her with everything she needed.

Dario had told her they would be staying for at least a fortnight as he had a series of meetings planned with his business contacts on the island. He was a busy man, and she knew she had a demanding job too. Although every time she tried to think about her job, the dark shadow lurking at the edge of her consciousness threatened, so she had decided not to worry about that. But if Dario had brought all this stuff with him, she would need more clothing, too. She didn't want to embarrass him with her paltry wardrobe.

'I've only got the hospital gown, and my negligee and this,' she said, sweeping her hands over the ensemble of slim-fit jeans, a camisole and linen shirt he'd already provided.

She sank her teeth into her bottom lip. Dario's lifestyle was extremely glamorous, way too glamorous for a woman with no luggage. No wonder she felt overwhelmed.

'Stop worrying, *cara*,' Dario said, his thumb glancing over her bottom lip.

She stopped biting it, the goosebumps going haywire at his tiny touch.

'There is nothing you need that isn't already purchased.'

'But I didn't bring...'

'The cases are mostly yours.' He swept his hand to encompass the luggage still being transported by several burly men to the fleet of cars. 'Della, my PA, assured me it was all you would need.'

Megan gaped, feeling like Alice, having just plopped down the rabbit hole.

All she would need? There was enough luggage here to dress the entire catwalk at Paris Fashion Week.

'But I... I'm not sure I can afford it,' she said, desperately trying to scramble out of the rabbit hole, and plant her feet on solid ground. Or solid*ish.*

'Shh... Do not concern yourself with money.' He captured her chin, forcing her gaze away from the never-ending parade of designer suitcases. The slow sexy smile that spread across his handsome face wasn't any less disturbing. 'I can provide what you need while we are here.'

She knew he was just being thoughtful again, but the insistence in his voice brought back the flutter of frustration. 'That's very generous of you, but I prefer to pay my own way.'

In the hospital, he'd told her she was his responsibility, and, while she'd found it comforting then, it was way past time she let him off the hook now. She still had some interesting bruises—her back was covered in them, which made her sure she must have fallen down his stairs. Obviously, he'd taken the whole responsibility thing too far because she'd had her accident in his home—which was touching, but it was getting a bit over the top.

'I certainly don't think you should pay for my clothes. I can do that.' Of course, she wasn't sure she could pay for those clothes, because from the logos on the bags they looked way out of her price range. 'You must let me pay you back.' *Once I've secured a loan.*

Dario's brows furrowed, the offer clearly confusing him. Obviously Giselle hadn't been much of a pay-your-own-way kind of gal. Maybe she didn't have Giselle's supermodel face and figure, but she did have financial integrity. And an unimpeachable work ethic.

Or at least she thought she did.

One of the luggage handlers arrived to tell them everything was ready.

Dario replied in Italian, instructing them to take the luggage to the house and have the housekeeper unpack it in the bedroom.

She got momentarily fixated on the word *bedroom*, his rich, resonant voice making it sound ludicrously seductive.

The thought of what they would be doing together in the bedroom in the coming days, and possibly for two whole weeks, cheered her up considerably.

She couldn't wait to get started. Her body's constant hunger for Dario, the desire to feel his touch again—the one thing about their engagement that was straightforward and uncomplicated. Maybe she wouldn't need to wear all the clothes. Then she could return a few and get a refund.

'Come, we will talk about this on the drive,' he said.

'Okay,' she said, although she couldn't see what else there was to discuss.

But then he put a palm on the small of her back, caressing the base of her spine, to direct her to the car—and she had to bite her lip to hold back the purr.

As the car sped down the track towards his magnificent home on the clifftop, an infinity pool came into view nestled amid trellises of flowering vines as the road climbed towards the house.

'The clothes are a gift, Megan,' he said, in the velvet-over-steel voice she recognised as the one he used when instructing his employees. 'I am a very rich man. I enjoy purchasing things for you. Payment is out of the question. Do you understand?'

'Um…okay?' she said, because she was distracted by that delicious voice, and the thought of all the things they were going to be doing in his *camera* tonight.

The villa was beautiful. But she didn't get much chance to examine the sweep of living and dining rooms on the ground floor, before Dario had directed her to the second floor and a suite of rooms with a terrace that offered an awe-inspiring view of the pool and the terraces of lemon groves that led down to the sea.

The men carrying her luggage trooped in behind them.

But all Megan's attention was on the enormous bed. The four-poster, draped with gauzy muslin curtains, was the room's focal point, both romantic and exciting and a tiny bit intimidating. Her heartbeat throbbed in her throat— and a few other key parts of her anatomy.

'Megan, this is Sofia,' Dario announced and she turned to find a tiny bird of a woman in her fifties with lush chest-nut hair standing beside him. 'She is the villa housekeeper and in charge of all the staff; she will take care of your needs. I have instructed her to serve you your meal in your rooms tonight, so that you can rest.'

'*My* rooms?' she asked, confused now. Wasn't this suite of rooms for both of them? Where was Dario planning to sleep? 'But…?' Her cheeks coloured. How could she ask him such an intimate question in front of all these people? 'Won't you be joining me?' she managed at last.

'Not tonight, *piccola*,' he said.

He cupped her face and gave her a proprietorial kiss on the forehead, making her feel like an over-eager puppy. 'You must rest. And I must work.'

He dropped his hands and stepped back so quickly she might almost have imagined the perfunctory peck, but for the prickle of sensation on her cheeks left by the calluses on his palms. '*Buonanotte*, Megan. I will see you tomorrow, at suppertime.'

At suppertime?

He marched out of the room, his back ramrod straight. What about the rest of the day?

She stood in the centre of the beautiful room, feeling dazed and desperately disappointed.

Sofia chatted away in a halting mix of English and Italian about how overjoyed they all were to have their boss's *fidanzata* in residence, while directing a couple of maids to fold away the dazzling array of designer clothing and making menu suggestions for Megan's evening meal. But as Megan watched Dario, tall and indomitable, disappear down the steps of the terrace, she'd never felt less like a *fidanzata* in her life.

CHAPTER ELEVEN

'*Buongiorno, Sofia. Dove Dario?*' Megan asked the house-keeper, hoping she'd got her tenses right—and trying not to be embarrassed by the all too familiar enquiry. Because she'd been asking the housekeeper every morning for almost a week where Dario was that day.

'*Buongiorno, signorina.*' Sofia smiled, busy stretching and pulling the fresh pasta dough, as she did every morning. '*Il capo?* He is with the fishermen, today,' she said. 'Tonight we will have *Pesce spada.* How you say that in Inglese? Swordfish? Yes?'

Megan nodded as her heart sank to her toes.

The swordfish season had started that morning. She had spotted the traditional long boat with its twenty-five-foot mast from the veranda in her suite of rooms as the sun turned the deep blue sea a ruddy pink.

So Dario had got up at dawn and would no doubt be gone all day. Again. She had hoped today, with no business scheduled that she knew of, he might be able to stay at the villa.

'*Delizioso.*' She did a smacking action with her lips and Sofia laughed.

'Only if the fish smile on us,' the housekeeper said. 'If they do not we have sardine ravioli.'

Megan smiled back, but it felt forced and tight.

She adored Sofia. The woman was friendly and efficient and had been happy to spend the afternoon yesterday teaching Megan how to make fresh tagliatelle, which had gone a long way in keeping her anxiety at bay. But she didn't think pasta making was going to cut it today.

She'd been at the villa for nearly a whole week now. And each day had begun to blend into the next. At first she'd forced herself to appreciate the chance to rest and heal, and had tried not to let Dario's absences from the villa—and indeed her bed each night—upset her.

The villa was in a stunningly beautiful location with every possible luxury at her fingertips and Sofia, along with her two young maids, Donella and Isa, were more than happy to accommodate Megan's every whim. She'd made herself relax and enjoy the late mornings spent lazing in bed or sitting on the veranda with strong coffee and a tray of Sofia's fresh pastries; the light lunches spent lounging by the pool reading the books she'd downloaded from the Internet; the afternoons spent swimming and exploring the secluded coves, picking wildflowers, and trying to identify the local fauna. It had all helped to fill up the empty hours and stop her from obsessing about getting the chance to talk to Dario. About their engagement. And about all the things she could not remember about him.

To be fair, the complete lack of any stress had been welcome at first, as her body healed from her accident.

She also called Katie using Skype each afternoon, but that had become an exercise in avoiding all Katie's probing questions about how everything was going with Dario.

In the last few days, she had tried to be content seeing Dario each evening, when they would sit down to the lavish four-course meal Sofia and her helpers prepared each day.

Last night, as the citronella candles burned, illuminating his harsh, handsome face, Megan had watched her fiancé devour Sofia's delicious food and finally drummed up the courage to ask him about himself.

But he had directed the conversation away from anything personal, and in the end she was just so pleased to see him, she had decided not to push.

The hunger inside her, though, had been like a dragon, breathing fire into every single erogenous zone, as she'd watched Dario's firm sensual lips consume a mouthful of Sofia's light, tart lemon zabaglione. She thought she'd caught his dark hooded gaze on her cleavage, but it had flicked away again so quickly she wasn't sure if she had imagined it.

Her confusion and desperation had increased as he had escorted her once again to her suite of rooms and bid her goodnight at the door. So much so that she had been unable to hold back the suggestion that he spend the night with her.

She'd waited patiently for him to make the first move. But her patience was at an end now. Instead of taking her up on her offer, though, he'd said nothing at all, his jaw rigid.

So she'd ended up babbling on about how much better she felt now and if she relaxed any more she'd turn into a narcoleptic... A very fat narcoleptic, because Sofia's cooking was to die for.

For a split second she thought she'd seen the flare of desire, burning even hotter than her own, but then he'd politely refused her offer and walked away—leaving her breathless, anxious, and hopelessly frustrated.

And now this.

After waking up feeing tense, confused and even more frustrated this morning, she discovered he'd gone again.

It was too much.

Ordinarily, she did not have a confrontational bone in

her body—that had always been Katie's forte. But after over a week of rest and recuperation at Dario's command she didn't think she could survive another night alone without exploding.

Bidding Sofia good day, she returned to her rooms and rifled through the swimwear she had found among all the other clothing. She picked out a stunning scarlet bikini, which she had shied away from wearing because of the purpling bruises on her hip and back. But the bruises were as good as gone now.

She squeezed herself into the two swatches of red Lycra, dismayed to discover that whomever had bought the clothing had underestimated Megan's bust size a fraction. Either that, or Sofia's pasta blow-outs had added a cup size.

Didn't matter. Dario needed to see the evidence for himself—that she was fully recovered from her accident. It was way past time she demanded more of his time and attention.

She packed her e-reader, some sun lotion and a towel into her beach bag, and headed to the two-tiered pool situated on the terrace below the villa, prepared for a long wait. Dario would have to walk up through the lemon groves from the harbour and past the pool when he got back from his fishing expedition—by which time she would be more than ready to confront him. She hoped.

Dario trudged up the last few stairs through the lemon grove, calculating the hour as close to four o'clock. He would wash the fish smell off, then take the Jeep over to Matteo Caldone's farm, to check on the new irrigation system he'd financed for Matteo's groves of blood oranges. His shoulders ached from reeling in fish for ten straight hours. And he was ready to collapse. But after last night, he was not about to risk seeing Megan any sooner than was absolutely necessary.

After today's back-breaking work, surely tonight he'd be able to sleep without being visited by the erotic visions that had woken him hard and aching every night since they'd arrived.

Walking away from her last night had nearly killed him. Once he'd returned to his own room, he'd had to resort to the sort of self-servicing that he hadn't indulged in for some time.

Unfortunately, it hadn't done much good. He'd woken sweating and swearing, with images of Megan on their one torrid night together turning his hunger into a ravening beast.

The salt air, perfumed by the tart, citrus scent of the lemon grove, filled his lungs. He let it go, the heavy sigh almost as weary as his aching body. Tonight he would sleep and he would not dream of Megan. Those high, full breasts with their pale, pink peaks as she begged for...

He blinked and wiped the layer of sweat off his forehead.

Dio! Basta!

Then he rounded the drystone wall that led to the pool terrace and all the air left his lungs in a rush. Sitting on a sun lounger, her wet hair tied on top of her head in a loose knot, her full breasts barely covered by the world's tiniest bikini, was the star player in every one of those erotic fantasies.

A small voice in the very recesses of his brain was whispering that he should step away, disappear behind the wall and then trek across the fields to approach the villa from the other side, before Megan spotted him standing there like a besotted teenager getting his first glimpse at a nude centrefold.

But he couldn't move, the blood powering down to his groin silencing that small voice while making the rest of his body scream in agony.

Then her head rose and she saw him.

Too late.

'Dario, I've been waiting for you,' she said. Or that was what he thought she said, because it was hard to tell over the sound of the blood plummeting out of his brain to destinations south.

Standing up, she walked across the sun-warmed terra-cotta tiles towards him, her gorgeous curves threatening to spill right out of the minuscule patches of scarlet fabric with each seductive sway of her hips.

After getting up at dawn to spend an entire day hauling fish so he could get a stranglehold on his libido, everything south of his belt buckle had lost the plot in less than a second. The throbbing ache in his groin was now even more pronounced than the aching pain in his over-tired muscles.

Next time I see Della I am going to murder her. What was she thinking, ordering Megan that pitiful excuse for a bikini?

'I need to speak to you about…' She paused. 'About what happened last night… I don't want to spend another night alone, Dario. I understand that you are busy, that you have work commitments. But there are so many things I need to talk to you about and I've hardly seen you since we arrived.' Her voice drifted through his mind but he could make no sense of what she was saying.

Was that excuse for swimwear actually *wet*? He could see the clear outline of her nipples through the fabric.

Madonna! Please kill me now.

Her conversation drifted into one ear and then right out of the other as he became fixated on taking each of those ripe, responsive peaks between his lips and torturing them until she begged for release.

'Dario, are you even listening to me?'

'*Scusami?*' he mumbled, forcing his gaze back to her face. Her pale skin had acquired a healthy sun-burnished glow in the last week, her cheeks now a bright scarlet hue even more tempting than that damn bikini. He wanted to lick that fluttering pulse in her collarbone so much he could almost taste her sweet, spicy aroma on his tongue.

The way he had every night in his dreams.

Her eyes widened. Was that trepidation or shock he could see in them, the misty green bright with stunned knowledge? Then she rolled her lip under small white teeth and everything inside him shattered. All the smart, practical, moral reasons why he couldn't taste her seemed to explode in a cloud of nuclear fallout.

'Stop biting your lip,' he said, his voice a low husky croak he barely recognised as his own.

'Dario! Don't speak to me like that.'

He wrapped his hands around her upper arms and hauled her to him.

Her eyes popped even wider as his heat and hardness rubbed against her naked belly through confining denim.

Then all coherent thought fled as his lips landed on succulent skin and his hands captured the lush curves that had finally pushed him over the edge into madness.

Megan sucked in a shocked gasp, the pulse point in her neck battering her collarbone as Dario bent his head to press his mouth to her neck.

Everything burst inside her, all the hopes and needs and wants that had been escalating for days.

Pulling free of his controlling hands, she plunged her fingers into his thick hair, and dragged his face up.

He wanted her too. She hadn't imagined it. She hadn't.

The truth felt like a sunbeam, bursting inside her, as hunger darkened his hot blue eyes to black.

'Kiss me,' she demanded.

His tongue thrust into her mouth as he massaged her bottom, notching the apex of her thighs against the mammoth ridge in his jeans.

She almost wept for joy, kissing him back for all she was worth, her heart ready to explode right out of her chest.

He held her easily, forcing that thick ridge against the one place where she needed it the most. A guttural moan seemed to reverberate in her chest. Was that her or him? Did she even care?

The pleasure mounted, her whole body on fire now, her melting core seizing into greedy knots of desperation, coiling tighter and tighter.

She wanted him inside her, but before she could think or talk or even respond the wave crashed over her in one titanic surge of pure unadulterated bliss.

She tore her mouth from his, her broken cry shattering the harsh grunts of his breathing.

He swore suddenly and let her go, his eyes still turbulent with need. But instead of taking her back into his arms the way she wanted, the way she was desperate for him to do, he looked stunned.

'Don't stop,' she begged. 'Please don't stop.'

Her chin and cheek stung from the rough abrasion of his stubble. Her whole body shuddered from the force and fury of the spontaneous orgasm.

'I should not have touched you,' he said, his voice brittle.

'Why not?' What was he talking about? 'I wanted you to,' she added, in case he hadn't realised it. But surely he must have realised it. She'd had a climax from little more than a kiss, for goodness' sake.

She felt herself flush at the gaucheness of that. But she refused to care. Why should she be embarrassed by her wildfire response to this man? They were a couple, engaged to be married.

He raked his hands through his hair and took another step back. Why did he look so tortured? 'This cannot happen.'

'Why not?'

'I…' He hesitated, and for the first time ever he seemed unsure of what to say. 'I could have hurt you. I should not have put my hands on you.'

Oh, for— Not that again.

Temper, rich and fluid, and surprising in its intensity, rose up. 'I'm not made of glass, Dario. And I'm going to be your wife. I want your hands on me.'

He stared at her, as if he were lost for words. She could see the huge erection outlined by battered denim. Then he said, 'You have bruises still.'

'No, I don't. You can see, they're as good as gone.'

His gaze went all glassy again, before he suddenly jerked his head up.

'I smell,' he said, his voice a harsh croak now. 'I must wash off the scent of the fish.'

'You smell of the sea. And of you. Both scents that I love.' As much as she must love him in order to have agreed to marry him. Did he doubt her commitment to him? Was that it? Because she couldn't remember why and how she had fallen for him? But how could she know if he would share nothing of himself with her? Not even his body.

'Please don't do this,' she said, determined to find out why he was so reluctant to repair what seemed to be broken between them. 'Don't shut yourself off from me.'

She reached out a hand, wanting to stroke that rigid cheek, to reassure him. But he jerked back, out of reach.

'I must go and shower. I will be out this evening.'

'Why? Where are you going?' she asked, trying to stifle the bitter stab of rejection. And hurt.

'I have important business to discuss with Matteo Caldone, a local farmer... A new irrigation system. I will eat when I return, but don't wait for me.'

Before she could get in a word of objection, or shout at him that she did not want to wait any longer, he had marched past her and headed up to the house.

She stood by the pool, stunned by the encounter. But as she dug her teeth into her lip she remembered that flash of pure unadulterated need that had darkened his eyes to black before he'd swooped down on her, and she realised one incontrovertible truth.

The only way to bridge the huge chasm that had opened up between them was to get Dario back into her bed. Everything else would surely follow. Because wasn't that how they'd fallen in love in the first place? Through their shared passion for each other?

And if their mad kiss a minute ago had proved one thing above all others, it was that Dario De Rossi still wanted her as much as she wanted him.

All she had to do now was make him admit it.

There would be no more polite requests. No more sitting meekly every evening while he directed the conversation, staying obediently in the villa all day or standing silently while he gave her that one peck on the forehead and left her alone for another night.

The only way Dario would ever see her as an equal, the only way he would ever open up to her, was if she started behaving like an equal. And started demanding that he satisfy the hunger that was eating them both up inside.

No way was she going to let him run off to yet another crucially important meeting. A crucially important meeting she was fairly sure he had made up on the spot.

Rushing over to her bag, she stuffed everything inside. She dashed across the pool terrace and headed towards the villa.

Time's up, Dario. You're not running away from me again.

It took her ten minutes to find his suite of rooms in the opposite wing of the villa from hers. Rooms she had never been invited to. That was going to stop too. What was the point of her being here, if they spent no time together? She wanted to know everything about him—all the things she must have discovered that first night in order to have agreed to this engagement, but which she had forgotten about because of her accident.

She passed through a simply furnished but beautifully appointed office, equipped with all the things necessary to run a multinational business. That he'd had all this equipment installed in a holiday home gave her pause for a moment. Dario was a workaholic. But she had no idea why he was so driven.

Shouldn't she know about these parts of his life? She wanted to know why he couldn't settle, and what had turned him into a man so determined to succeed that he could never take a break.

She found the door to his bedroom closed. She knocked but there was no answer.

Gathering her courage, she pushed the door open.

A bed even bigger than her own stood in the centre of the room, but it had none of the romantic flourishes of hers. It suited him, she decided. The open shutters on high windows afforded him a glorious view of the cliff tops and the path leading towards the harbour. The room was enormous, but Dario was nowhere in sight.

Had he left already? Had she missed him?

But then she jumped at the sound of splashing water coming from a door in the far wall. She noticed a pile of clothes that had been discarded in a heap on the floor.

Her throat thickened, the eddying heat making the skimpy bikini feel tight and restrictive on her swollen breasts.

He was in the shower. Should she go and join him?

Vague memories of him naked and fully aroused, the muscle and sinew slicked with water from a different shower, blasted into her brain.

Don't overthink this. Just do it.

She knotted the summer wrap around her waist, and inched open the bathroom door.

Her breathing hitched, her heartbeat thudding against her ribs. The hot melting sensation detonated between her thighs and spread throughout her body like hot lava. Her knees shook, the sight before her bringing the dragon in her belly to scorching life.

Dario stood ten feet away in the walled shower, naked, with his back to her, the pounding of multiple jets of water meaning he hadn't heard her come in.

He had one hand braced against the mosaic tiles, his head bent, obviously concentrating on what his other hand was doing. Steaming water slicked down bunching muscles, making her throat close the rest of the way.

His masculine beauty was so breathtaking, each hard plane and muscular bulge so perfectly sculpted, it staggered her.

He was pleasuring himself. Heat flushed through her. Had their kiss done that to him?

What a waste.

'Dario?'

His head whipped round and the hot blue gaze locked on her face. His motions stopped. He turned as his hand fell away and her gaze dropped to the huge erection standing proud against his belly.

'You should leave,' he said, but the command in his voice was tempered by the rasp of longing.

She shook her head, unable to speak. Or move. Everything inside her gathered into that harsh, aching desperation to feel the thick length buried deep inside her again. Because the one thing she could remember with complete clarity was how glorious he could make her feel.

He turned fully now, allowing her to look her fill. He was magnificent. Moisture pooled in her sex, dampening her bikini bottoms.

'If you do not leave, I will have you,' he said, his voice so husky she could barely hear it against the beat of the water. 'Is that what you want?'

'Yes.' She found the strength from somewhere, even though her whole body was trembling now with desire and longing.

He nodded, his jaw hardening. His eyes took on a harsh glint that was both terrifying and exhilarating in its intensity. 'Then prove it to me.'

Wrapping long fingers around the hard shaft, he stroked himself—not fast this time, but with agonising slowness. The erotic display was almost more than she could bear.

'Take off your clothes for me,' he said, the tone harsh with demand.

Undoing the knot on the belt with clumsy fingers, she obeyed him without question. The wrap slid off her shoulders, the silk feeling like sandpaper as it whispered over her sensitive skin.

'All of it.' The commanding tone tightened the desire in her gut. 'I want you naked.'

She reached behind to undo the hook—unable to deny him now even if she had wanted to. The scarlet triangles dropped from her breasts, and the swollen, tender flesh burst free from its confinement. The breeze from the open window tightened her nipples into hard, aching peaks.

He dipped his head, still stroking that huge erection, to indicate she must lose the bikini bottoms too.

She plucked the tie on one side, and the fabric dropped away.

She couldn't breathe—anticipation warring with panic—as he finally released his erection and turned off the water. Wrapping a towel around his hips, he walked towards her.

Gripping her face, he forced her gaze to meet his and stroked his thumb across her cheek. 'Are you scared of me, *piccola*?' he said.

The nickname stirred a new memory of their first time. She had been a little scared then, of his size and what was to come, but she wasn't scared now.

'No,' she said.

'Then why are you shaking?'

'Because I want you so much,' she said, knowing if there was one thing she was sure about, this was it.

He swore, but then said, 'I want you too. Very much.'

Bending, he scooped her up and carried her quaking body out of the bathroom and into his bedroom. Another memory assailed her, of being in his arms before. Of being carried up the stairs in his penthouse... Bright, exciting, arousing. But something darker tickled at the edges of her mind. Not in his penthouse, but her apartment, the crunch of broken glass under his feet...

The shadow she had been avoiding lurched into view and she slammed the door shut on that memory.

Don't go there. Concentrate on the wonder of now.

Placing her on the bed, he dragged off the towel, releasing that magnificent erection. Reaching past her, he found a condom in the bedside cabinet and rolled it on.

She folded her arms over her breasts as he climbed onto the bed.

'Don't hide from me, Megan.' He moved her arms above her head, bracketing her wrists in one hand.

She cried out as he circled one swollen peak with his tongue, then nipped at the tip. The exquisite spike of sensation darted down to her already molten sex.

He played with her breasts, circling and sucking, releasing her wrists to stroke her slick folds.

Her moans turned to sobs of need, deep and guttural, almost animalistic as he circled and caressed, right at the heart of her.

He raised his head, releasing her tortured nipples, his erection prominent against her thigh. 'I must taste you. It has been too long,' he said.

'Yes,' she heard herself beg, not sure if he was asking her permission but desperate for him to know he had it.

Parting her thighs, he held her bottom, then knelt between her legs and lifted her. She arched, offering herself to him as his stubble brushed against her inner thigh. His hot tongue licked at the heart of her, delving and exploring.

Her sobs turned to ragged pants, the pleasure coiling tighter and tighter. His mouth found the pulsating nub at last and suckled hard.

She cried out his name as she shattered, the orgasm crashing over her in undulating waves.

He licked her through the last drops of her climax, as if gathering her taste. Then he let her go, to settle on top of her. Capturing her hips, he thrust deep in one shudder-ing glide. She stretched for him, the pleasure returning in a titanic rush as he rocked her back to orgasm with stag-gering speed.

His hands anchored her, forcing her to take the full measure of him. His penis butting that perfect spot he had found once before. The second orgasm swept through her, obliterating everything in its path—the trail of fire sear-ing through her from her head to the tips of her toes. She clung to his shoulders, her broken sobs matched by his shout of release as he followed her over at last.

It felt like a month but could only have been a few sec-onds before she returned to her senses, every part of her aching with the exhaustion of a body well used.

He shifted, still so huge inside her. And then lifted his head.

Why did he look so guarded? Surely he must know he'd just given her a multiple orgasm.

'You are okay?' he asked. As if he really didn't know.

'Are you kidding?' she said, even though she could see he was deadly serious. 'I'm spectacular.'

The deep chuckle—although slightly strained—was like music to her ears.

'Are you sure I did not hurt you?' he murmured.

'I told you, I'm not fragile,' she said. 'I love having sex with you. I really, really love it.'

His eyes narrowed, but the shadows retreated as he cra-dled her cheek and then kissed her nose.

'Ditto,' he said. Then he rolled off her.

She felt the loss of his warmth, his heat, immediately. Was this the moment when he told her he had to leave, to go to his irrigation ditch meeting? She was all ready to protest, to finally demand that he stay with her for the rest of the day. But instead of getting out of the bed, he hauled her close, wrapping his arms round her, and tucking her against his body, her back to his front.

She could feel the hard length of him nestled against her backside.

'You're not leaving to go to the lemon farm?' she asked tentatively, afraid to remind him of the engagement.

'It is an orange farm. But no, not tonight,' he said.

He leaned over her to grab his smartphone off the bedside table. Then keyed in a text.

Snuggling against her back, he nibbled kisses along her shoulder. Incredibly, after that shattering orgasm—make that two shattering orgasms—she felt the sleeping dragon wake again in her belly.

'Are you hungry?' he asked.

Talk about a loaded question.

'Yes,' she said.

'What are you hungry for?' he asked, and she could hear the smile in his voice.

'For food and for you, not necessarily in that order.'

The deep chuckle reverberated against her, sending a ripple down her spine as he cupped her breast and played with the nipple. The arrows of sensation shot straight back to her still tender sex.

'Sofia will leave us food in the kitchen for later. But first you must rest.'

The tenderness in his voice, and the feel of his thumb teasing her nipple, made her feel warm and languid, but far too turned on.

'Why must I?' she asked.

She didn't want to sleep. She'd had over ten days to sleep and now she finally had him where she wanted him, why would she waste time sleeping?

'Because you will need your strength for what I plan to do to you next.'

She shifted around, so she could look over her shoulder to gauge his expression. 'Really? You're going to make love to me again?' She could hear the eagerness in her voice and hoped she didn't sound like a nymphomaniac. But already the renewed stirrings of hunger in her belly were becoming unbearable.

Clearly satisfaction was a relative term, and, when it came to Dario De Rossi, she might never be satisfied.

He sighed against her hair. 'I have no choice. My will is not my own any more.'

It seemed a strange thing to say. Why would he choose not to make love to her, when he now had conclusive proof she was fully recovered from her accident?

Before she had the chance to debate the puzzling thought, or ask any of the many other questions that had tormented her about him, his hand slid off her hip, and sure seeking fingers found her sex, blasting into oblivion everything but the renewed surge of longing.

CHAPTER TWELVE

'CAN I ASK you a question?' Megan's eyes brightened, her voice eager, as she laid Sofia's antipasti onto an earthenware platter.

It was late, and Dario was ravenous. Unfortunately, it wasn't just for the array of cold food his housekeeper had left out for them.

How could he still want her? When he'd spent the last six hours with her in his arms—none of it catching up on the sleep he had lost in the last week.

He tore off chunks of the sesame seed bread Sofia made fresh each morning and added it to their midnight feast.

'You may ask,' he said, reserving the right to refuse her, the anticipation in her eyes making him instantly wary. He should never have touched her. He had promised himself he wouldn't. But ultimately he had been unable to stop himself from taking what she offered so eagerly. And now he would have to pay the consequences—by finding a way to deflect her curiosity again, without feeling like a bastard.

'There are so many things I want to ask you about that night.'

Dario carried the platter and their glasses to the moonlit terrace, the fresh scent of sea air and citrus fruit doing nothing to appease the clutching sensation in his gut.

Was her memory about to return at last? Perhaps the sex had finally jogged something loose?

'What do you wish to know?' he asked, cautiously.

Lloyd Whittaker had been charged and arraigned, thanks to Katie's testimony. He had been refused bail and would be standing trial in a few months. Megan hadn't mentioned him though, not since she had woken up in the hospital—convincing Dario her memory loss was centred exclusively on her father. If she asked about him now, it would surely mean her mind was finally healing as well as her body. But as she sat down opposite him at the table and began to serve them both from the platter, her vibrant hair the colour of rich red flames in the light from the citronella candles, he didn't feel as pleased at the prospect of her memory returning as he should.

Here was a chance to finally end this charade. To free them both from the obligations brought about by Whittaker's attack and Megan's subsequent amnesia.

But as he watched her tuck into Sofia's *verdure misti*—clearly considering what she wanted to ask very carefully—his mind spun back through the events of the past week. Against all the odds, and despite the knife-edge of sexual frustration that had been driving him insane for days, he had looked forward to seeing her each evening.

At last she looked up from her plate. The sheen of olive oil on her lips made them look even more kissable than usual. Dario licked his own lips.

This was just sexual desire, nothing more. His hunger for her was clouding his usually crystal-clear judgment. Anything she wanted to know he would be happy to tell her—because it would bring her memory back sooner and that was what he wanted.

'Would you tell me about yourself?' she said.

Anything except that.

His shoulders tightened. 'What do you wish to know?' he said, stalling.

She smiled shyly, the subtle shift of her lips as sexy as it was beguiling. 'Everything. All the things you told me that night about your hopes and dreams and where they came from.'

'But I told you nothing.' He never talked about his past, his childhood, because it had no part in who he was now. He'd made absolutely sure of that, erasing all but the most basic facts about his life from the media narrative of his success.

'Don't be silly.' She seemed amused at his attempt to correct her. 'You must have told me something for me to have fallen in love with you.'

The happy expression on her face made his heart kick against his chest in hard, heavy thuds.

They weren't in love. He had never loved anyone—not since... He shut down the thought.

'I expect I told you loads of stuff too,' she added in that effortlessly optimistic tone. As if love were something you would want, instead of something that would only hurt you. 'But I can't seem to remember that either. So you're going to have to help me remember.'

But there is nothing to remember.

'I don't know what you would want to know,' he said, still stalling.

'Then how about I ask you all the things I'm curious about now, because that's probably what I asked before?'

He didn't know how to reply to that, but she didn't really give him much of an opportunity before she had launched into her first question. 'The article in *Forbes* said you grew up in Rome.'

'I grew up outside Rome, in one of the government-funded housing projects constructed for the Roma community,' he said, reluctantly. The snap of bitterness in his voice that he couldn't control, though, surprised him.

He'd realised a long time ago that the experience of waking up to the scrabble of rats outside the trailer window and the sound of his own teeth chattering during winters in the slum, or the fetid smell of rotting trash and effluent from the urinals that marked the summer months, were the very experiences that had driven his need to succeed. He'd long ago come to terms with the terrible privations of his childhood. He wasn't embarrassed or ashamed of his origins, but still he had no desire to revisit that time in his life.

'You're of Roma descent? That's amazing,' she said, as if this were something to be proud of.

He frowned. Didn't she know that the Roma people had been treated like the scum of Europe—ghettoised and vilified, their way of life stigmatised for generations?

'My mother was.' The information slipped out, as he recalled the woman who had been so proud of her heritage, despite the hovel they'd lived in.

'She *was*?' Sympathy and compassion clouded Megan's eyes, making the antipasti in his stomach threaten to revolt. 'I'm so sorry, Dario. Is your mother dead?'

For a moment, the memories threatened to flood in on him. Memories he had spent a lifetime forgetting. 'Yes, but it was a long time ago.'

'Oh, no, were you a child?'

'No,' he said, because he had never been a child, not in the sense she meant. Grasping his fork in stiff fingers, he scooped up a mouthful of Sofia's grilled aubergine. It tasted like chalk as he swallowed.

'What about your father?' she asked.

'I never knew him,' he said, the lie coming much more easily this time.

He heard a groan, and looked up to see Megan digging a knuckle into her temple as if trying to erase something from her mind.

'Are you okay?'

'Yes, but… It's like there's a darkness lurking at the edge of my consciousness and I don't want to let it in.' Had the question about his father made her think of her own? And all the things she was trying so hard to forget?

He got out of his chair. 'Then don't.' Smoothing the unruly hair back from her brow, he took her other hand, and tugged her out of the chair. 'It has been a long day. You must get some rest now.'

'Really, it's nothing. I'm fine.' She dropped her hand. 'It's gone now.'

'I insist. You must rest.' Despite her protests, he scooped her into his arms, the desire to protect her from the demons that might be chasing her foolish in the circumstances, but there nonetheless. He needed her to remember, but if remembering still caused her pain…

She gripped his neck, looking a little perturbed. 'Put me down, Dario,' she said. 'You're overreacting. I can walk.'

He tightened his grip, taking her into the house. 'Let me carry you. It is my fault you are over-tired.'

She held on to his neck and stopped struggling, but the look she sent him was one of frustration. He didn't care. He was right. They had overdone things because where she was concerned he was incapable of keeping his libido in check.

'I don't see how it's your fault when I seduced you,' she said, indignant now.

'That is debatable,' he said, but he couldn't help smiling at the stubborn lift of her chin, or the combative light in her eyes. He was beginning to discover how brave and spirited she could be, for a woman who had been brutalised. Unfortunately, it only turned him on more.

He felt the familiar response in his groin and took a turn once he'd mounted the stairs towards her suite of rooms.

'Stop right there. I'm not going to my own rooms,' she shouted, and all but threw herself out of his arms—a bit too brave and spirited for his liking.

He swore as he scrambled to gather her back up. 'Come back here.'

'No.' She batted his hands away.

'You need to sleep. You must do as I tell you.'

'I'll do no such thing. You have to stop treating me like a child, Dario. I'm a grown woman. I can make decisions for myself.'

He could feel his own frustration kicking in. 'Not when you make the wrong ones.'

Like believing even for a second you could have fallen in love with a man like me.

'Will you listen to yourself?' Megan propped her hands on her hips.

How could she want to kiss him and strangle him at the same time? Seriously though, they were getting this straight once and for all. No more excuses and no more distractions.

'This is not the nineteenth century and you are not in charge of me.'

'You need rest. It is past midnight and you have reached orgasm six times today,' he shot back.

So he'd been counting. Why did that make her feel so much better?

He crossed his arms over his chest, looking like the poster boy for stubborn manhood, strong and indomitable. He who should be obeyed at all costs.

Well, not by me, buster.

His biceps bulged deliciously beneath the short sleeves of his T-shirt.

Her sex clenched.

Fine, maybe some distractions were going to be impossible to ignore. But that didn't mean she was going to let him get away with his high-handed attitude a moment longer. They'd come so far this evening.

The sex had been awesome, but the tantalising glimpse of intimacy had been even more so. Because the few things she had discovered about him tonight had intrigued and moved her in ways she couldn't explain.

Who would have believed that beneath the charming, charismatic sex god lurked a man who could look stricken when he was asked about his mother? He'd masked it quickly, but she'd seen enough to be touched—and compelled to wonder about so many things. Things she hoped to be able to discover about him in the days ahead. But she couldn't do that if she allowed him to push her away again—to compartmentalise their time together and keep her at arm's length.

'And I enjoyed every single one of those orgasms,' she said, something rich and empowering surging through her when his face flushed with aggravation. Sex was the key.

She knew sex, even great sex, didn't necessarily translate into emotional intimacy—especially with a man who was so adept at hiding his feelings. But it was a very good start. Not to mention rewarding in its own right.

'But we wouldn't have been at it for six hours straight if you hadn't denied us both the pleasure of sleeping together for a whole week,' she added.

'You were recovering from your accident,' he said.

'And now I'm not recovering any more. I'm recovered. I think we proved that comprehensively this evening.'

Something flickered across his face again, before he looked away. She touched his forearm, felt it tense beneath her fingers.

'How about a compromise?' she murmured. She didn't want to argue with him.

'What compromise?' he said grudgingly.

She smiled, amused by the muscle bunching in his jaw. For a moment he reminded her of a petulant child, so used to getting his own way he had forgotten how to bend. Only he wasn't a child, not in any sense of the word. Because...biceps.

'This is funny somehow?' The muscle in his jaw started to throb.

She bit down on her lip, trying not to let loose the smile that wanted to burst over her face.

Because instead of finding his taciturn show of temper intimidating, she found it exhilarating...and unbearably arousing.

His gaze glided down to her mouth, and she felt the spark of awareness leap between them.

'Here's what I suggest,' she said, deciding to ignore his rhetorical question. 'I'll consider taking your advice about my welfare, if I think it's warranted, but only if you agree to let us start behaving like a couple.'

No way was she letting him confine her to her own bedroom again.

'What does that mean? We are already together here.'

'I want to share a bed with you.'

His eyes narrowed and she could see he was about to refuse, so she jumped in before he could.

'I want us to sleep together...' She hesitated. Would this make her sound too needy? She frowned. How could it when they were engaged? Since when did engaged couples sleep in separate rooms? 'I like being in your arms. I want to go to sleep with you and to wake up with you. It's important to me.'

Dario knew he should refuse. She did not know what she was asking. They weren't a couple.

But before he could force the words out, she said, 'You make me feel safe, Dario. I don't want there to be so much distance between us. Or why are we even considering getting married?'

The plea in her voice made him feel like a bastard. He should tell her now that the engagement had been a ruse. A ruse that had got out of control. But somehow, he couldn't bring himself to do it. Something about the way she was looking at him, as if he could harness the moon and the stars for her if she asked him to, made him want to say yes.

She trusted him. When she learned the truth, it would crush that trust. But until then, he wanted her to feel safe and secure.

He cupped her cheek, his heart thundering in his chest when she leant into the caress and smiled.

'I can accept that compromise...' he said, touching his thumb to her bottom lip. 'But only if you promise to let me seduce you when we get to my bed?'

Maybe it had been a mistake to deny them both the physical pleasure that flared so easily between them? Perhaps this physical closeness was what she needed to find the strength to battle the darkness lurking at the edges of her consciousness. And really, what better way was there to distract her from her foolish desire to get to know him better? Which was all part and parcel of her foolish delusions that she loved him—or had ever loved him.

She smiled, the quick grin captivating and full of mischief. 'Absolutely—assuming of course I don't seduce you first,' she said, batting her eyelashes outrageously.

'Dio!' He reached for her hand and marched towards his own bedroom. Her seductive chuckles spurred the aching hunger in his groin.

Somehow or other he'd completely lost the upper hand in this negotiation, but the feel of her hand in his—and the thought of having her in his bed tonight, all night—was like a heady drug, making it hard for him to remember why exactly he had ever insisted on keeping her out of it.

CHAPTER THIRTEEN

MEGAN SQUINTED AT the sun shining through the shutters and stretched, disappointed to find Dario's side of the bed empty. Again. After over a week of waking up in Dario's bed she still hadn't managed to wake up before him. Her body protested, the desire to slip back into sleep almost overwhelming. She yawned, forcing the tiredness back. And grinned. Too much spectacular sex could be exhausting.

As she rolled over onto her belly, her grin widened at the sight of Dario's smartphone on the bedside table. He couldn't be far, probably in his study next door catching up on emails while she slept the day away.

Thank goodness he hadn't left without her. He'd mentioned a speedboat trip to the lagoon on the other side of the island today—one of the many trips and excursions they'd been on ever since she'd moved into his suite of rooms.

She'd used her newfound boldness to insist he start taking her with him each day on his different trips. And although he'd been reluctant at first, she was so glad she had insisted—because she'd discovered so many amazing things, not just about the island but about Dario, too.

Isadora had only a small fishing village on the other side of the peninsula on which the villa sat, many of whose inhabitants had to commute to the mainland to find work.

Dario had invested a lot in rejuvenating the island's once thriving community—building a new dock, constructing the villa itself and resurrecting the old olive, lemon and blood orange groves that had once thrived in the volcanic soil and had been a mainstay of the island's economy.

Each day, Megan would discover a new aspect to everything he was doing on the island, as he oversaw those projects with her in tow.

For a billionaire with a portfolio of international companies and investments, Dario had no qualms about getting his hands dirty. And the islanders hero-worshipped him, while also being comfortable treating him like one of their own.

Maybe she hadn't made much headway getting him to talk more about himself, or his past, but everything else she'd discovered had only made her fascination with him increase.

He was still bossy, but she had begun to realise that was all part of how focused and intense he was. He would never ask something of someone he wasn't prepared to do himself. And maybe he was still guarded about personal information. But his focus and intensity each night in bed—and on the occasions when they snatched a chance to make love in the daylight—showed a care and concern for her pleasure that made her sure what they were forging together was much more than just a physical connection.

She could make him laugh, lighten that dark, brooding quality that had once intimidated her, but now made her love him all the more.

And today she had a plan. To make a much bigger dent in that wall he seemed determined to keep erected around his emotions. And her plan was simple. Today was the first day they would be alone for one of their excursions. She would seduce him into a puddle and then pounce on him while he was floating on a cloud of afterglow—unable to resist her brilliantly subtle interrogation.

Of course, her plan was a risky one, because up until now she'd been the one who could barely remember her own name after they made love. But today she planned to get sneaky.

She'd asked Sofia to provide a picnic for their trip—to lull Dario into a false sense of security and satisfy his boundless appetite for food—and she was going to wear her scarlet bikini—to torture him with his boundless appetite for her.

She picked up the phone on the table to check the time.

Nearly noon? She frowned. How could she have slept so late when she had something so important to do today?

Throwing back the cover, she sat up.

Mission: Puddle of Lust, here I come.

The nausea came in a rush, the wave heaving up from her stomach so suddenly she was already gagging as she raced into the bathroom. She made it just in time before she lost last night's dinner in the toilet bowl.

Finally empty, her stomach settled into an uneasy truce as she sat on the cool tiles. Her whole body ached as she reached to push the flush button.

'*Cara*, what happened? Were you sick?'

Dario knelt down beside her and wrapped her robe around her shoulders to cover her nakedness.

'Yes, I think I must have picked up some kind of bug.' She placed a hand on her stomach. 'Although it feels a bit better now I've been sick.'

'Has this happened before?' The fierce expression made her heart bobble in her chest. Why did he look so disturbed? She hoped he wasn't going to use a little bit of nausea as an excuse to start treating her like an invalid again.

'No, not really.'

'No or not really?' he said.

Her stomach had been a bit queasy yesterday, and the day before when she'd woken up. But she hadn't been sick. And it had soon gone away. His brows drew down as he waited for an answer and she decided a white lie might be in order.

'No, it hasn't happened before.' Using the toilet bowl, she pushed herself to her feet, steadfastly ignoring the pitch and roll of her not-completely-calm belly.

She tied the robe around herself and brushed her teeth, before walking past Dario, who still looked concerned.

She escaped into the walk-in closet.

'I'll be fine,' she said, her voice deliberately light and cheery. 'All I need is a swim in the lagoon to make me feel better. I'm sorry I slept in so long.'

But when she came out of the closet, he'd disappeared into his office. She heard him talking in rapid Italian on his smartphone. She tuned it out. Thank goodness, he'd found some business thing to keep him occupied. She slipped on a summer dress and sat at the dressing table to slick on sun cream and a touch of lip gloss.

But when Dario returned to the bedroom, his face was still set in the same unforgiving lines. 'How is your stomach?'

'It's wonderful. Really, I'm great now. How long will it take to get to the cove?' she asked, still trying to inject as much brightness into her voice as she could, while subtly changing the subject.

'We're not going to the cove. The helicopter will be ready in ten minutes, to take us to the hospital in Palermo.'

The forbidding expression had her already dodgy tummy jitterbugging. 'Don't be ridiculous. I'm not going to hospital over a bit of nausea.' Why was he overreacting?

'Tell me, Megan,' he said, his jaw so tense she wondered he didn't break a tooth. 'Have you had a period since we arrived?'

'No,' she replied.

'Then we must go to the hospital for a pregnancy test.'

Shock came first, her stomach jumping right into her throat. 'But I can't be pregnant, we've used condoms the whole time. It's not possible.' It couldn't be possible. Except... The evidence started to reel off in her mind: her increased bust size, the tiredness and now her upset tummy. But more than that, something else niggled her memory.

Sofia tapped on the bedroom door. 'The helicopter is waiting, *signor*. Do you still want the picnic?'

The nausea charged back up Megan's throat at the mention of food.

'*No, grazie*, Sofia,' she heard Dario murmur as she shot back into the bathroom.

CHAPTER FOURTEEN

'YOU ARE INDEED pregnant, *signora*.' Dr Mascati smiled benignly at Megan. Dario tensed beside her, his expression as guarded as it had been throughout the never-ending helicopter ride from Isadora to the heliport on the roof of the exclusive private maternity centre.

'Are you sure?' Dario said, his voice curt. Not angry but not happy either.

Megan understood. This was shocking news. No wonder he'd hardly said a word to her since they'd boarded the helicopter. She hadn't known what to say either. However whirlwind their engagement, they hadn't even talked about their wedding yet, so introducing a pregnancy into that was bound to put huge pressure on them both.

But after the last week, the last two weeks, ever since waking up in the hospital, she'd come to terms with why she had agreed to marry him in only one night. Maybe it was mad. But the more she discovered about him, the more she got to know him, the more sure she was that she could love this man.

'The test is unequivocal,' the doctor said in his perfect English. 'There can be no doubt. We can do a scan in a couple of weeks so you can see your baby for yourself.'

'Okay,' she murmured, acknowledging the leap of joy despite her shock.

She placed a hand on her stomach, imagining the tiny life growing inside her. However unprepared for this they both were, this pregnancy felt so positive on some elemental level.

Perhaps it was her hormones talking. Or the endorphin high she'd been riding on for the last seven days. But whatever it was, she knew instinctively that despite the challenges and problems ahead they would be able to deal with them.

Maybe it had only been a few weeks, but Dario—so protective, so caring, so solid and sure of himself—would make an amazing father, and she... She would do everything within her power to be the mother this tiny life deserved.

Dario spoke to the doctor in rapid Italian, but the conversation floated somewhere over Megan's head as she caressed her invisible baby bump. And tried to contain the secret smile in her heart.

Dario was obviously unsure about this development; she could tell that already from his reaction to her sickness, which she realised now had been panic. Pure and simple. She just hadn't recognised it as such, because he always seemed so confident and commanding. But once they were alone together, they could talk about his misgivings. This pregnancy didn't have to be a bad thing.

'Megan, we must go now.' Dario's words jolted Megan out of her reverie.

'Oh, yes, thank you, Dr Mascati,' she said, trying not to sound too spacey. Even if she felt as if she were flying somewhere above the cosmos at the moment.

Dario rested an arm around her waist to guide her out of the doctor's office. They made their way back up to the roof, Dario gripping her hand as they crossed the heliport to the waiting chopper. He said nothing, his face now an implacable mask.

She stared out of the window on the flight back. The noise of the chopper's blades made it impossible to speak and she was grateful for that, because she wanted to get her thoughts together. He would need reassurance. Understanding.

But she was confident he would come around to the idea given time and encouragement. If he was sure enough of his feelings to ask her to marry him after only one night, no way would he be too scared to take on this responsibility once he knew how positive she was about it.

The sun dipped towards the horizon as they swooped over the villa and came into land on the cliff-top heliport.

Dario led her back to their suite of rooms in silence. Sofia arrived to lay out a meal for them on the terrace. The housekeeper sent her a gentle smile and Megan smiled back at her. Did she know already?

She stared out at the sea, the sky lit in a redolent array of red and gold and deep darkening blues. Isadora was such a beautiful place. What a wonderful place this would be to bring up a child.

No, that was silly, Dario had a life in New York, and so did she. But surely they could spend summers here— with their baby. She had to tell Katie. Her sister would be an auntie.

'Eat, Megan. You must be hungry.' She glanced back to find Dario watching her. She dialled down her excitement.

She was getting way ahead of herself. There was still so much to talk about. So much to discuss. She mustn't try and second-guess Dario's feelings. The doctor had said the pregnancy was still in the very early stages.

'Yes, of course,' she said, although the truth was she was far too nervous to eat. 'This looks delicious.' She picked up her fork and forced down a few bites of the aubergine and cherry tomato pasta she was sure Sofia had produced for her delicate stomach on Dario's orders.

'Do you want to talk about the baby?' she asked, as nonchalantly as she could, while she watched him closely, to gauge his reaction.

The impassive mask cracked, revealing something she didn't understand until he said, 'It is not a baby yet. It is a collection of cells.'

The flat words tore into the excitement that had buoyed her up through the helicopter ride.

Her fork clattered onto the plate. 'I know I'm only a few weeks pregnant, but...' She stalled, suddenly scared to say what she thought.

'But what?' he asked, not unkindly.

'It feels like a baby to me,' she managed around the feeling of dread suddenly pushing against her throat.

What would she do if he wanted her to have a termination? She hadn't even considered that option. Wasn't sure she could go through with it even if that was what he wanted. Had she been foolish, expecting him to be as happy about this unexpected event as she was? Probably, yes.

'Don't you want this baby?' she managed to say. Prepared for the worst, but desperately hoping for the best.

He looked away, across the terrace towards the sea, the breeze lifting the thick waves of his hair, lost in thought for a moment. But when he turned towards her, his gaze was shadowed and unreadable. 'That is not my decision. It is yours.'

The bright bubble of hope burst at the pragmatic tone.

Her hand strayed back to her tummy, and she looked down at the still invisible bump. Tears stung her eyes. She blinked furiously, desperate not to let them fall. It was just all so overwhelming. Not only the news about the baby, but how she felt about Dario. If she chose to have it, would it tear them apart? And if she chose not to, would it tear her apart?

Courage, Megan.

Dario was right: this was her choice to make and she'd already made it. She had to stand up for this child, and hope that, however early it was, this pregnancy wouldn't destroy what she was just starting to build with Dario.

Wiping away the errant tear that had slipped over her lid, she forced her gaze to his and smiled at him. 'I want to have your baby, Dario. Very much.'

He stiffened, and for once she could see his feelings written plainly on his face. He didn't look upset by her response—or particularly pleased either. He simply looked stunned.

He dipped his head, the nod almost imperceptible. 'I see,' he said.

She clasped her hands in her lap, but she couldn't stop her fingers from trembling, the emotion pressing on her chest too huge to deny as the bridge they had spent one glorious week building felt as if it were collapsing into a yawning chasm.

He didn't want this baby. She could see it in the rigid line of his jaw, the shadowed distance in his eyes.

'Dario, please tell me how you feel about it,' she begged, using every ounce of the courage she had left as another tear slid down her cheek.

He shook his head, then reached over to brush the tear away. The tender gesture made her heart ache even more.

Pushing back his chair, he stood up. 'You are tired, *piccola*. We can discuss this tomorrow.'

She should say something, anything—they needed to discuss this now, before he had a chance to retreat even further into that protective shell—but the last of her courage deserted her when he lifted her into his arms.

She clung to him as he carried her into their bedroom.

They would make love, she told herself desperately. That would make everything better. They were always so close when they made love.

He undressed her, but when she thought he would reach for her, he didn't. Instead he brought her one of his T-shirts, and helped her into it.

'Why do I need this?' she asked.

'Because your other nightwear tempts me too much,' he said. 'You need sleep, *cara*.' He tucked the thin sheet around her and stood up.

'Aren't you coming to bed, too?' she asked.

'Not yet, I have some work to do. I will be in later.' He kissed her forehead. 'Go to sleep. It has been an exhausting day.'

She wanted to argue with him, but her limbs were already melting into the bed. She curled up, taking in the comforting scent of sandalwood that clung to the sheets.

It was okay. She was still in his bed. And he would be back soon. Then they would make love. And all their differences would melt away.

'Don't be long,' she murmured as her eyes drifted closed.

But he had already left the room.

CHAPTER FIFTEEN

'SHE'S PREGNANT? FROM the look on your face, I'm guessing that's not good news,' Jared said, his voice as dispassionate as usual over the scratchy Internet connection.

Dario rubbed his forehead, trying to erase the picture lodged there of Megan crouched on the bathroom floor retching this morning. And the single tear drifting down her cheek this evening in the dusk as she told him she wanted to have his child.

He was shattered, the strain of trying to keep his emotions in check the whole day too much even for him. He had called his friend to get some advice. Even though he knew already, there was no advice that would fix this.

'No, it's not,' he said. 'It happened on our first night. We had agreed she would take the morning-after pill, but now she doesn't remember that conversation.' He raked his hand through his hair, and stared out into the starry night sky, the full moon reflecting off the bay.

The shock of this morning's discovery had left him reeling. He couldn't become a father. And Megan did not want to be a mother—something she would know when her memory returned. But as that hadn't happened, the way forward now was fraught with complications—and heartache.

And the last week had only complicated the situation more. It was all his fault.

He should never have given into his hunger for her and taken her back into his bed. And he should never have agreed to her requests to accompany him during the day. Because the time they'd spent together, instead of reinforcing all the reasons why they could never be a couple, had done exactly the opposite.

He'd become completely enchanted with her. Not just her enthusiasm and responsiveness in bed, but the way she behaved out of it.

He'd come to adore the bright, eager and surprisingly well-informed chatter about all the improvements he was making to the island. He'd been charmed by the way she had captivated the local fishermen with her faltering Italian or bonded with Matteo Caldone's wife over how to make gnocchi. And had come to rely on having her with him, having her by his side. She had made even the most tedious details of his working life an adventure. When he'd woken up this morning, he'd been stupidly excited about the prospect of taking her for a swim in a lagoon, knowing how much he would enjoy seeing her wide-eyed wonder at the cove's natural beauty. In the space of one short week, she'd managed to turn him into someone he didn't even recognise. Someone fun and playful and optimistic in a way he hadn't been in years. In short, a besotted fool.

But worse than that, in the past week, their fake relationship had started to feel real. Real enough that even the thought of her giving herself to another man had begun to torture him. And he had forgotten to be cautious and careful with her feelings as well as his own.

But this morning's bombshell had brought that illusion crashing down around his ears.

This relationship wasn't real.

He could never love Megan—however much he had enjoyed her companionship in the past week or the intense physical connection they shared. And Megan didn't really love him, because any feelings she had for him were based on a lie. But even knowing all this, when she had stared at him out of misty green eyes and told him she wanted to have his child, for one terrifying moment he had actually wanted it to be true.

It was all such a catastrophic mess, and he didn't know how the hell to get them both out of it.

'So she still doesn't remember that you were never engaged for real?' Jared said.

Dario shook his head.

'Maybe it's time to tell her the truth and see what happens, pal.'

Jared was right, of course. He should have said something tonight when he'd had the opportunity. Should have said something a week ago, before he'd taken her back into his bed. But still he kept second-guessing himself.

'What if I do that and it only confuses her more?' A tiny, foolish part of him almost wished she never regained her memory. It just went to show how far he had lost his grip on reality.

'Doesn't seem like you have much of a choice,' Jared said. 'It's either that or she has the kid and you pretend to love her for the rest of your life.'

'No, that is not an option, either.' His head felt as if it were about to explode, the fear that had haunted him since childhood making his heart kick his ribs in harsh erratic thuds.

'Sorry I can't be of more help, man,' Jared said, sounding as dejected as he felt. 'Good luck.'

Signing off, Dario turned off his laptop and walked back into the bedroom.

She lay curled on the bed, having kicked off the sheet. Her body looked small and defenceless as she moved restlessly in her sleep. He should sleep elsewhere, but as a small moan escaped he found himself taking off his clothing and slipping into the bed. He cradled her quaking body in his arms, and inhaled the flowery fragrance of her hair. Her breathing deepened as he stroked the soft strands to quieten her and the arousal that was always there became a dull ache in his groin.

'Shh, *piccola*,' he murmured as he struggled to find his own peace. And a way out of this mess—without hurting the smart, sweet, beautiful woman he had come to know.

'You stupid slut! You're worse than your mother.'

The darkness came to her in dreams, seeping into her consciousness where she couldn't defend herself against it. She saw her father's face contorted with rage, sweat dripping down his mottled skin as he screamed at her.

Pain rained down on her, striking her shoulders, her back, lancing through her heart, shattering everything she had ever known about herself and her place in the world.

'You're not mine! You and your sister were whelps from her lovers.'

Her broken sobs echoed in her head, as she begged her daddy not to hurt her any more. But her daddy wasn't her daddy now, and he hated her.

Just as the pain became unbearable, Dario's voice beckoned her out of the nightmare. 'Shh, Megan, it's okay, I'm here, you're safe.'

She awoke with a start in the darkened bedroom with Dario's arms around her.

Shapes formed in the moonlight. Familiar, comforting shapes. Dario's face harsh with concern. The giant bed where they had slept together in each other's arms. Luxury furnishings gilded by the light of the waning Mediterranean moon. The citrus and sea scented breeze brushed her naked skin through the open shutters. And for a moment she did feel safe. Secure. Loved... So happy.

But then the darkness unfolded as the dream returned. Not a dream this time though, but terrible reality: the kaleidoscopic colours of the ballroom as Dario spun her around in a circle on their pretend date; her sobs of fulfilment as he stroked her to orgasm; the wry tilt of his lips as they discussed emergency contraception; the shuddering humiliation as she received her father's text.

Nausea pitched and rolled in her belly. Clammy sweat covered her body. And horror hit her hard in the chest.

'*Cara*, are you okay?' he said, his voice gentle, coaxing.

But she knew the truth now. And his concern, his care, wasn't love. It was pity.

She could feel the phantom pain from her father's belt and see the dispassionate concern so clearly on Dario's face as he knelt next to her shattered body.

'Let me go.' Pushing against his hold, she wrestled with the cloying sheet, climbed off the bed.

'What's wrong?' he said, pulling back the sheet to follow her.

She scrambled away from him, her back hitting the wall of the bedroom, the cool plaster chilling her fevered flesh. 'You lied. Why did you lie to me? We were never engaged!'

For a moment he looked shocked, but then she saw the guilty flash of knowledge. Her thundering heart felt as if it were being crushed in her chest.

'Your memory has returned?' he said, his voice patient. And tightly controlled.

She gagged. Rushing into the bathroom, she heaved what little she'd eaten the night before into the toilet bowl. As she carried on heaving she heard him enter the bathroom behind her.

A dim light came on and warm hands settled on her shoulders.

She spun out of his grasp. 'Don't touch me.'

He stood in sweat pants, his magnificent body mocking her. How ridiculous she had been, to think for even a moment that a man like him would ever love her.

He had been nothing more than a glorious one-night stand—was never meant to be more than that—and because she had lost her memory, he had spun out a lie.

But why? Why would he do that?

He lifted a hand. Like a man trying to calm a frightened beast. 'You are over-emotional. Come back to bed so we can talk.'

She shook her head, trying to hold on to the tears making her sinuses ache. 'How could you pretend we were engaged? That we were in love? For all this time? Why would you?'

It had all been a lie. How could he justify it to himself? And how could *she*? She'd fallen in love with an illusion. None of this had been real. Her hand strayed to her stomach and the baby growing there. None of it except her child.

The child he didn't want, and now she knew why.

'You are overwrought. You need to calm down,' he said.

Anger flared. She clung onto it desperately, through the heartache and the weariness. 'Don't patronise me. Tell me the truth. Why did you tell me we were engaged? Why did you make me believe you loved me?'

He stiffened at the use of the word. And her already battered heart cracked silently in two.

'I never pretended to love you,' he said, and the last remnants of hope that she hadn't even realised she still clung to withered and died. 'I wanted you to get well,' he said. 'Which is why I brought you here. Away from the press, the trial, so you could recover. It was for your own good.'

'You slept with me, knowing I didn't know the true nature of our relationship. How could that be for my own good?'

His eyes darkened, his jaw tensed, and she felt the spark of electricity arc between them. She folded her arms across her chest, her swollen breasts tender and far too sensitive under that searing gaze. The T-shirt he had helped her into before bedtime suddenly felt see-through, every inch of skin prickling with the need to feel his touch as memories of that first night, of the past seven nights in his arms assaulted her.

'You offered yourself to me,' he said. 'And I should have resisted. But everything we did together we both enjoyed.'

It sounded reasonable, persuasive even. And of course, he was right. She had begged for him to make love to her. Except it had never been love. At least not for him. 'Did you ever care for me at all?'

'Of course I did,' he said, the frustration in his voice helping her to bury the agonising hurt deep.

'And what about the baby? Perhaps you should tell me how you really feel about that now.' But she already knew, the bitter truth turning her insides to jelly.

He heaved a deep sigh. Seeing the agony in his eyes made her want to weep. 'Megan, it is complicated. You must see that? Now you remember everything?'

He stepped forward, but she threw up a hand. 'Please don't, don't come any closer.' She couldn't stay strong, stay invulnerable, make any sense of this if he touched her. The chemistry between them had messed with her head all the way down the line. And made her fall in love with a phantom.

'My father attacked me because he hated me.' She pushed the words out past the thickness in her throat. The cruel, ugly words her father had said striking her all over again with more viciousness than the belt he'd used on her. 'He pretended to care about us for years because of the money in our trust funds. But this...' she swung her hand between them '...what you did, feels so much worse.'

Dario dragged a hand through his hair, cursed under his breath. 'I understand you are angry and upset,' he said. 'But let us talk about this in the morning. It's the middle of the night. You're tired. Come back to bed. I can make you feel better.'

'You think sex will make this better?' she said, stunned.

'I think it cannot hurt,' he said.

The wry twist of his lips made her heart shatter at her feet. That he had manipulated her with sex wasn't really the point, because she had revelled in her own destruction. That he thought it would make things better now, though, almost made her feel sorry for him.

How could anyone have such a jaundiced view of love and relationships that they thought sex was the only connection worth having?

He approached her.

But she held up her hand. 'No. I don't want to sleep with you, Dario.'

Of course, they both knew that wasn't strictly true. She only had to be in a room with him for her body to prepare itself for him. To yearn for him. It would be humiliating if it weren't so sad.

But she refused to give in to the yearning. She had to guard what little was left of her heart. In the hope that, one day, she would be able to heal. And move on from this.

'I need to think,' she said as her mind raced. She had to get away from him. Get away from Isadora. If for no other reason than to protect her child. 'I want to return to my own room.'

For a moment she thought he looked stricken at the suggestion, but it could only be an illusion like everything else. She had never been able to read him, or his feelings; her emotions had played tricks on her in the last few weeks, but that was the biggest trick of all.

She moved past him into the bedroom, pathetically grateful when he made no move to stop her. Her whole body began to shake, heat flushing through her, when she glanced at the bed, the rumpled sheets a testament to her foolishness and naiveté.

She had spent her whole life trying to please her father, a man who had never loved her. And if her memory hadn't returned, she might have done the same thing again with Dario.

'We will speak of this again in the morning,' Dario said from behind her. 'And find a solution.'

She turned around as she reached the bedroom door. The red fingers of dawn had begun to lighten the sky outside, shadowing his handsome face, and her heart squeezed tight in her chest. For just a moment, he looked like the loneliest man on earth.

'I never meant for you to be hurt,' he said.

The last tiny flicker of hope guttered out as she acknowledged something incontrovertible. Maybe he hadn't meant to hurt her, the way her father had. But the truth was he had.

She left the room as one of the tears she had promised herself she wouldn't shed slipped over her lid. She scrubbed it away with her fist.

After returning to her bedroom, she kept the exhaustion and the heartache at bay to dress.

She called Katie on her cell, and tiptoed out of the house, then rushed through the lemon groves down to the harbour, where the fishermen would be setting out for their morning catch.

As she stood on the deck of a small fishing boat, the aroma of fish and sea salt made her delicate stomach revolt. She retched over the side of the boat, but there was nothing left to throw up. As she raised her head she caught sight of the villa spotlighted on the hilltop in the early summer dawn.

She imagined Dario inside. And all the hopes and dreams that had never been real. Letting them go would be the hardest thing of all. But she had no choice.

While she had been falling hopelessly in love with a fantasy, he had managed to seal himself off from any emotion that would make him vulnerable.

So now she had to do the same.

Dario awoke, the pounding on his bedroom door disorientating him for a moment. He sat up, confused to find the other side of the bed cold. Then the details of the argument just before dawn came back to him.

He swore viciously, trying desperately to ignore the treacherous memory of Megan's face, white with shock and grief. And worse still, the deep sinking hole in his stomach when he had been forced to let her leave, and had lain in his empty bed alone.

But then he registered what his housekeeper was shouting through the door.

'Signor! Signor! La signorina e andato, ha lasciato con I pescatori.'

Megan has left with the fishermen? What the...?

He leapt out of bed, dragging a robe on as he raced to the door to find Sofia on the other side looking distraught as she explained in frantic Italian what she had heard from the young man delivering that morning's fish.

Dread spread through him. Megan had left? She had hitched a lift in a fishing boat in the middle of the night?

When she was still dealing with the emotional trauma of her memory returning? When she was pregnant? Was she mad?

He charged down the corridors until he reached her suite of rooms—to find the bed empty and unslept in, and a note addressed to him perched on the bedside table.

He picked it up, and flicked it open.

Goodbye, Dario.
I will take care of a termination.
Please don't contact me again.

No, no, *no.*

The note dropped from his numbed fingers and fluttered down onto the carpet.

He should have been relieved, he should have been grateful, that she had come to her senses, was going to do the sensible thing. But he felt none of those things as he clutched his head in his hands, and slumped onto the bed.

The cold, hard lump of devastation and grief in the pit of his stomach dragged him back to another time. He forced his mind to shut down as he lifted his head to stare out of the window at the new summer day, the dawn light spreading over the ocean.

And wondered if he would ever feel warm again.

CHAPTER SIXTEEN

Two months later

MEGAN SAT IN the chauffeur-driven car and watched the phalanx of photographers and reporters charging down the steps of the Manhattan courthouse towards them. Her sister, Katie, gripped her hand.

'Are you sure you're okay to do this, sis?' Katie's voice vibrated with the strength and maturity that she had gained ever since Megan had returned from Isadora.

Megan squeezed her sister's hand. 'We both need to do this to make sure Lloyd Whittaker stays behind bars as long as possible.'

The clamour outside the car became deafening as two burly security guards muscled their way through the crowd and one of them opened the driver's door.

He leaned into the interior. 'We have a detail to see you safely into the courthouse, Miss Whittaker. You both okay to go?'

The harsh flash of halogen lights blinded Megan as they stepped out of the car and were muscled into the courthouse, the noise becoming deafening as the reporters shouted questions.

'Are you here to testify against your father, Miss Whittaker?'

*'Megan, tell us about your affair with Dario De Rossi?
Are you two still an item?'*

She clung to her resolve, tried to tune out the mention
of Dario's name, to keep her nerves steady. But as they entered the main foyer she saw the tall, lean figure of Dario's
friend Jared Caine standing beside the security checkpoint.
And her heart careered into her throat.

'Well, if it isn't Mr Tall, Dark and Patronising,' Katie
said, in a sing-song voice shot through with sarcasm as he
walked towards them. Katie hadn't mentioned Jared before
now, but she had never played nice with guys who told her
what to do, so her animosity towards Dario's friend didn't
really surprise Megan.

'Hello, Miss Whittaker, Katherine,' Jared said, in the
confident, impersonal tone she remembered from the only
other time she'd met him. If he'd heard her sister's jibe,
he didn't let on.

'Why are you here?' Megan asked, anxiety gripping
her insides.

'Dario's giving evidence at the moment,' he replied.

The news she had been dreading sliced through the defences she had been putting in place ever since running
away from Isadora. But she maintained eye contact with
Dario's friend, determined not to give away the turbulent
emotions churning in her stomach.

She'd known this was likely. She'd just have to deal
with it.

It didn't matter if she wasn't ready to see him again.
He'd done what she'd asked, and hadn't contacted her since
she'd left Isadora at dawn.

It didn't matter that she hadn't been able to stop thinking about him. Or stop going over every minute, every second she had spent with him since that first night. It was a
weakness she would have to get over. Eventually. And it

seemed today was the day when she was going to be forced to confront it. And him. For the first time.

She needed to move on from the time they had spent together on Isadora. To accept that it had all been fake. The way he obviously had. Coming to terms with the truth about their relationship as well as the truth about her father—or rather her ex-father—would eventually make her a stronger, more resilient person.

If only she weren't going to be forced to take that next step today, of all days.

One of the security guards who had helped them into the building appeared to Jared's right. 'What's next, boss?'

'Stick around. Miss Whittaker and her sister will need an escort when they leave the building,' Jared replied.

'Did Dario arrange the bodyguards?' Megan asked and Jared nodded.

The protective gesture was like a new knife through the heart—and her hard-fought-for composure. She didn't want any evidence that he still cared, when he had never cared enough.

'Please, tell Dario we don't need his help,' she said.

The tension in Jared's jaw drew tight. 'You should tell him yourself. He's not exactly rational where you're concerned.'

What did that mean?

But before she could ask, the prosecutor's intern appeared looking harassed. 'Miss Whittaker, you're up next. We need to get you into the courtroom.'

Her stomach continued to rebel as the intern ushered them through the security line, leaving Jared behind.

As she walked into the courtroom her gaze immediately connected with Dario on the witness stand. Her steps faltered, the blast of heat not nearly as disturbing as the pressure on her chest as his gaze swept over her.

From a distance, he looked as indomitable and intimidating as ever, the tailored designer suit, clean-shaven jaw and close-cropped hair a far cry from the intense and yet tender, even playful, man she had glimpsed on Isadora.

Her hand strayed to her stomach, but she forced herself to let it fall away as the intern directed her to the front of the courtroom and the seats behind the prosecutor's table.

But she couldn't take her eyes from the man on the witness stand. And as she drew closer, for a moment she thought she saw a flash of pain and longing in those pure blue eyes.

She broke eye contact, the pressure on her chest becoming unbearable.

You're wrong. Stop deluding yourself.

She needed to cut out that fragile, foolishly optimistic corner of her heart that still believed she loved him, or that he might have grown to love her.

She pressed her hand to her abdomen. She had her child to protect now. The child still growing in her womb.

The child she could never tell Dario about, because he had made it clear he had never wanted it, or her.

How can it still hurt so much to look at her?

Unable to detach his gaze from Megan's, Dario blanked out the defence attorney's questions.

But then Megan's gaze dropped away from his. And he felt the loss all over again, as he had so often since that fateful night on Isadora when her memory had returned and he'd seen the pain he'd caused in those expressive emerald eyes.

She looked pale and drawn in the tailored skirt and jacket. Had she lost weight? Her wild red hair was ruthlessly tied back. The style should have made her look severe and unapproachable—but only made her look more fragile and vulnerable to him.

His fingers clenched on the varnished wood of the witness box as he forced his attention back to the defence attorney. He had to concentrate on his evidence—as the man continued his campaign to convince the jury that Dario had been the one to attack Megan and not her father—and ignore the agonising parade of regrets that had plagued him since that night.

Stop trying to remake the past. She ran from you. And rejected your child. This was the outcome you wanted. Why can't you learn to live with it?

But then the defence attorney's mouth twisted in a grim approximation of a smile as he delivered a stream of questions that smashed into Dario's already faltering composure like physical blows.

'You maintain that you have never hit a woman, Mr De Rossi? That it is simply not in your make-up to do so? But is it not correct that you come from a family with a history of violence against women? That in fact your father was an extremely violent man, who hit you and your mother on numerous occasions? And that you indeed witnessed him beat your mother to death at a very impressionable age?'

Megan's head jerked up as the court broke into uproar—the barrage of questions, and Dario's shocked reaction to them, tearing away the stranglehold she had around her own heart.

Oh, please don't let it be true. Please don't let him have suffered like that.

Her chest imploded, the information delivered by the lawyer too traumatic to contemplate. But then her heartbeat rammed her throat in hard, heavy thuds as she registered the devastation on Dario's face—the mask of indifference ripped away to reveal the true horror of what he had once endured, clear for all to see.

And suddenly all the unanswered questions that had plagued her since that night, the questions that had made it so hard for her to move on, slammed into her all over again.

Why had he been so determined to protect her? How could he have made love to her with such passion, such purpose, and felt nothing?

Dario remained speechless, and utterly defenceless as the prosecutor's attempts to halt the line of questioning were dismissed by the judge.

'Mr De Rossi must answer the question. The prosecution can determine the relevance of this information in due course.'

The court fell silent, Megan's heart shattering.

'I did not consider him my father,' Dario said in a voice hoarse with raw emotion. 'The man was a monster.'

'Indeed,' the defence attorney said, the word laden with theatrical doubt. 'And yet it appears you resemble him in no small degree. Is it not the case that you seduced Lloyd Whittaker's daughter to secure a business deal? That you attacked her when she tried to return to her father? That you spirited her away while she had no memory to your private island in the Mediterranean? And then discarded her when she had outlived her usefulness to you.'

Dario's eyes met hers, the guilt and regret now so clear and unequivocal, the shudder of yearning and love that flowed through her was beyond her control.

'I did not leave Megan,' he said, the resignation in his voice destroying her. 'She left me.'

The poignant words pierced her heart. And the tug of war she'd been playing with her feelings for Dario was comprehensively lost.

Why had she run from him? Why hadn't she given him a chance? Given herself a chance?

What she had found with Dario on Isadora might have been built on a lie—but why hadn't she even considered staying and trying to make it real? Had what she thought was strength been nothing more than cowardice all along?

'Perhaps we should ask ourselves then why she would run from you, Mr De Rossi?' the defence attorney continued. 'And why she would choose not to inform you that she carries your child? Is it because she is terrified of what you might do to her?'

Megan leapt to her feet, her hand cupping her stomach, the puzzled shock on Dario's face at the news she still carried his child making the guilt lance through her.

What had she done to him? This man who had strived to protect her? The way he had no doubt once strived to protect his mother? All the lies he had told had been to protect her fragile mind from its own fears until she was ready to face them. But the lie she had told him had been to protect herself. Because she had been too weak, too scared, to admit she loved him. And now he was being crucified because of it.

'Stop, please stop,' Megan shouted. 'It's not true. Dario would never hurt me.'

Noise exploded around her, the judge's gavel echoing in her head.

'Meg, are you okay?' Katie's fingers gripped her arm as the surge of emotion threatened to choke her.

She swayed.

Her gaze remained locked on Dario's as he jerked to his feet in the witness box.

She heard the judge's call to order, the prosecutor's shouted demands for a recess next to her ear, but the blood buzzing in her head became a cacophony. Her knees dissolved as she dropped into the dark.

'I have you, *cara*, you are safe now.' Dario's voice beckoned her out of the darkness and into the light, as it had once before.

The clean, spicy aroma of soap and man enveloped her. The noise still surrounded her, but she was in his arms again as he shouldered his way through the crowd, protecting her from the shouted questions, the press of bodies, the bright flash of lights.

The sound of a door slamming cut out the noise until all she could hear was her heart hammering against her ribs.

They were alone in a cramped office, the large desk pushed into a corner surrounded by shelves loaded with leather-bound books.

The July sunlight shone through the window, lighting the dust motes in the air.

'Can you stand?' he asked.

'Yes, I think so.'

He put her down, holding on to her waist until he was satisfied she was strong enough to stand unaided.

'It is true?' he asked, his gaze focused on her belly, his fingers gliding over the barely visible bulge. 'About the baby? It still lives?'

She nodded. 'Yes, they... They think it's a girl.'

'Una bambina?' he said, the sound so full of stunned pleasure her guilt began to strangle her. *'Bellissima.'*

'I'm so sorry I lied to you in my note. It was cowardly and unforgivable and I—'

'Shh, *cara*.' He brushed the tears away with his thumbs. 'You are not the coward. I am.'

'Maybe we were both cowards,' she ventured.

His lips curved in a sad smile that melted her heart. 'I think, yes.'

She blinked, feeling the salty sting on her cheeks. 'Is it true, Dario? What he said happened to your mother?'

Dario stared at the woman in front of him, so brave, so bold, so beautiful. But the earnest question ate into the joy at the news their baby still lived.

He wished she hadn't heard about his mother, wished she would never have to know the truth of his past. But how could he tell her any more lies?

Guilt consumed him, not just for his part in his mother's death, but for his part in Megan's assault. A part he had never truly acknowledged to himself until now.

Maybe he hadn't been the one to wield the belt, but his actions had left her vulnerable. Left her at the mercy of a violent man—the way he had once left his own mother at the mercy of another violent man.

He stepped back, letting his hands fall from her waist. 'Yes, it is true. She died and it was my fault.'

'How could it be your fault?' Megan said, the sympathy and compassion in her eyes making him hate himself even more.

'I provoked him. My father.'

'I don't believe you,' she said, her dogged defence of him making him more determined than ever that she should know the truth. The whole bitter truth about who he was.

'And even if you did,' she added, 'it still wouldn't make what he did your fault.'

'You do not understand,' he said. 'He was a powerful man. A rich man with another family. He called me his gypsy bastard, and my mother his whore.' That the memory of his father's taunts still haunted and humiliated him only made him feel more ashamed. 'He enjoyed hurting her. When I woke that night, I saw him on top of her. And I could see how terrified she was.'

'Oh, Dario.' She touched his arm. 'No child should have to endure that.'

He shook his head, planted his fists into the pockets of his trousers, his insides churning with the long-forgotten memories—the hollow aching guilt that would never go away.

'I shouted at him to leave, to never touch my mother again. I was eight years old, nothing more than a proud, angry boy, and I thought I was man enough to protect her. He was furious. He lost all control, began to beat me with the belt he had used on me before. But this time, I don't think he would have stopped. My mother saved me. She fought him with the last breath in her body. She died protecting *me*.'

'Stop it.' Megan gripped his arms and shook him, her fierce expression forcing him back to the present, and away from the gut-wrenching guilt of memories. 'Don't you dare blame yourself. You were a child when your mother died. Do you understand me? And she died protecting you, because she loved you.'

He tried to absorb what she was saying. But he could not, because he knew his mother's death wasn't the only guilt he bore. History had repeated itself with Megan. Just as the defence attorney had implied.

He grasped her cheeks, looked into that brave face and forced himself to admit the final truth that he had been trying to deny for so long.

'Don't you see, Megan? I did the same thing to you. I lied to you to get you into my bed that night. I lied about my intentions towards your father's company. All I thought of was my own pleasure. And you paid the price. My actions provoked Whittaker, in the same way my actions once provoked my father.'

She reached around his waist and pressed her cheek into his sternum. 'Please stop it, Dario. It's not true. You mustn't blame yourself for what my father did to me.'

He placed his hands on her shoulders, wanting to believe her, yearning to hug her back, but terrified of all the emotions rushing to the surface. All the emotions he had spent two months struggling to comprehend.

She smiled up at him, the tender expression making his ribs ache, and his whole body feel as if it were perched on the edge of a precipice.

'I love you, Dario. So much.'

Gripping her cheeks in trembling palms, he pressed his forehead to hers, wanting to plunge over the edge, as the last of the walls shattered around him.

But how could he ever deserve her, or their child, after all that he had done?

'You cannot love me,' he said on a broken breath. 'I do not deserve it.'

Folding her arms around Dario's neck, Megan kissed him, tears streaking down her cheeks now. She had to make him believe her, had to make him see that he was worthy of her love.

At last, he opened for her and took her mouth in a deep, seeking kiss. She felt the emotion shuddering through him. And into her.

She loved him. And she suspected he loved her too. But he'd been too scared to acknowledge it to himself, let alone her, because of what had happened to his mother. She understood that now. She had to show him that he didn't have to be scared of love any more.

She drew back, taking in deep breaths as she saw the

torment still shadowing his eyes. 'Do you love me, too, Dario?' she asked. 'Do you want this baby?'

He sighed. 'Yes. And yes.' He rested a hand on her stomach as her heart filled with happiness. 'But I could not bear it if I hurt you again.'

She pressed her palm over his, hearing the raw emotion in his voice.

This was a struggle for him. A struggle that would take time and work to heal all the way, but knowing he loved her, and knowing where his anguish came from—knowing why it had been so hard for him to acknowledge his feelings—was surely the start of something magnificent. Something they could build a future on, with their baby.

'Dario, I know you're scared,' she said. 'And now I know why you're scared.' Because he had been traumatised by his mother's death as a child.

Her heart would always break for that little boy—who had learned to cope with the trauma by persuading himself he did not deserve to be loved.

She took a breath, her whole heart now lodged in her throat.

'I'm scared too,' she said, determined to get through to that little boy. 'Everyone is scared when they fall in love. Because love is a scary thing. But it's also a joyous, wonderful thing. And to have the joy, you have to overcome your fear. Can you do that, for me?'

'But what if I make a mistake?' he said, still unsure. Still scared. 'What if I cannot be a good father? A good husband? What if my love for you and our child is not enough?'

'There aren't any guarantees. Life isn't like that.' She gripped his hands, the love flowing through her so strong now she thought her heart might burst. 'And believe me—considering how new and untried this adventure is for both of us…' she smiled '…we're both going to make mistakes. The truth is we're probably going to make a ton of them. But it will be okay. As long as we make them together.'

He looked down at her belly. 'But I don't even know how to be a father. My own father was a monster.'

'And my mother was a woman who cared more about her next orgasm than she ever did about her daughters,' she replied, her smile widening. 'Look at it this way— however rubbish we are at this, we'll already be so much better than them.'

He nodded and let out a hoarse laugh, which had a wealth of bitter knowledge in it. 'This is true.'

'So what do you say, Dario De Rossi? Are you willing to go on this adventure with me?'

Her heart stopped beating, it simply stopped, as she waited for him to answer.

'You are sure you want to go on this adventure with me?' he said, the seriousness in his face making her heart jump and pound in her throat.

'Absolutely.'

He nodded again—the fierce passion that flashed into his eyes as he drew her into his arms choking off her air supply.

'Then I don't believe I have a choice,' he murmured against her hair. 'Even I cannot continue to be a coward in the face of your bravery.'

She wanted to laugh, the joy bursting in her heart almost more than she could bear.

He clasped her cheeks and lifted her head. 'I think now we must make this engagement real,' he said. 'Will you marry me, *piccola*?'

Her heart soared. 'Absolutely.'

His mouth swooped down to devour hers, the giddy

contentment making her head spin as warm hands cupped her bottom, and heat spread through her.

A loud thumping pulled them apart as Jared's voice came through the door. 'Sorry, folks, adjournment's over. And the judge is getting antsy.'

'Stall them a minute more,' Dario shouted back. Then he turned to her, his expression sober. 'Are you strong enough to take the witness stand after me?' he asked, searching her face for any signs of fatigue or fragility. 'If you are not, I will make them wait until tomorrow.'

'No. I can do it. I *want* to do it,' she said, knowing she was strong enough to do whatever it took to put the man who had pretended to be her father behind bars—because with Dario by her side, she was strong enough to do anything. 'For us.'

Cradling her head in his hands, he kissed her forehead, then her nose, then her mouth—the play of his lips full of sincerity and hunger.

'For us,' he vowed.

EPILOGUE

One year later

'Shh, *bambina*, *Papa* is here now.'

Megan stretched on the bed and plumped the pillows behind her as she watched her husband walk back into their bedroom, having retrieved their crying daughter from her crib in the room next door, which had once been his office.

She smiled as the baby quietened, happily settling into her favourite place in all the world, nestled on her father's shoulder as he rubbed her back with one large hand.

The little diva.

At six months old, Isabella Katherine De Rossi had her father—billionaire master of industry and feared corporate raider—wrapped firmly around her tiny little finger.

'She is not wet.' Dario frowned. 'Could she be hungry again?' he asked, rocking his daughter gently as he returned to their bed.

Megan yawned, and looked out of the bedroom window to gauge the time by the Mediterranean sun, which was barely creeping over the horizon. 'No,' she said. 'She had her morning feed less than half an hour ago.' Megan couldn't contain her grin at the confusion on Dario's face.

He was still sometimes unsure about his role as a husband and father, and so fiercely protective of them both it

often led to him being a bit overzealous when caring for
Issy. He was always the first to pick her up if she cried.

'Do you think she is unwell?' he said.

'I think she just likes having you hold her,' she said.
'And she knows that if she cries, you'll rush in there to
pick her up.'

The frown eased from Dario's face and he chuckled as
he lay down on the bed beside Megan. Lifting his daughter,
he bounced her in his arms. The baby's delighted chuckle
joined his deep laugh.

'You are a bad *bambina*,' he said, rubbing her nose
against his own, the tone the opposite of chiding. 'You
mustn't scare *papa* like that.'

He settled back, with the baby curled on his broad chest.

With her head tucked under her father's chin and her
small fist stuck in her mouth, Issy dropped into sleep, secure in the knowledge that her father would hold her safe
in his arms.

'Dario,' Megan said, smiling as Dario turned towards
her. 'I need to talk to you about something.'

She'd held it off long enough. Had waited until they
were on Isadora again, where the pace of life was slower,
less pressured.

The last six months, heck the last year, had been idyl-
lic. She'd never imagined when they'd made that commitment to each other, in the dusty clerk's office during her
father's trial, that her love for Dario and their child would
eventually become so overwhelming, so all-consuming.
And because she'd been so content—and maybe also a
little scared that this adventure was still so new and fragile, especially for Dario—she hadn't wanted to make any
demands.

He'd changed so much though, from the cautious,
guarded man she'd known. He'd been to therapy to help

him deal with the lingering trauma of his mother's death. And they'd made a life for themselves in New York—in the huge brownstone he'd bought a block from Central Park. Their wedding had been a quiet affair on Isadora, with only the islanders and a few of his business associates as guests, plus Katie and Jared as witnesses.

Since their marriage, and even more so since Issy's birth, Dario had cut back on his business commitments, happy to spend long evenings and lazy weekends with her and Issy rather than building his business empire. Not that he wasn't still driven and focused, but he was now equally driven and focused about making his personal life as much of a success as his professional one.

And the bond he had established with his daughter was something that filled Megan with joy and wonder and gratitude every single day.

So the time was right to tell him about the interview she'd had last week in Brooklyn while their housekeeper Lydia Brady had looked after Issy. She'd held off and held off telling him about it, because she'd been concerned about his reaction.

Oh, just say it, Meg. For goodness' sake.

'Hmm...?' he murmured as he continued to stroke his daughter's back.

'I've been offered a job.'

His hand stopped moving as his head jerked round.

Well, that had certainly got his attention.

'A job where?'

'It's a charity in Brooklyn that administers a series of refuges for battered women and their children. They need someone to set up and then operate a new computer system to reduce the amount of time and money they spend on paperwork so they can spend more of it on setting up new refuges.'

He didn't say anything, but she could see the tension in his jaw. Instead of replying, he suddenly sat up and got off the bed.

'Dario? Where are you going?' she asked.

But he didn't turn to look at her, he simply walked out of the room mumbling, 'I should put Issy back into her crib.'

Okay, well, that didn't go according to plan.

Megan's heart sank as she flopped back onto the pillows, her excitement turning into a tangle of anxieties in the pit of her stomach. She didn't want to have a battle with him about this. But it looked as if she might have to.

Dario placed his daughter in her crib, and stroked the soft fluff of red hair on her head.

He wanted so much to say no.

He wanted to tell Megan she couldn't take the job. He didn't want her travelling to Brooklyn every day. Working for a charity that he could probably buy and sell several times over. He could fund the place himself. Throw money at them so they wouldn't need her computer expertise. If she needed a job, he could find her one at Whittaker's, preferably one that didn't require her to leave their house.

He wanted to insist that her daughter, their daughter, needed her mother at home. Where she would always be safe. And as their daughter grew, he would want to do the same thing to Issy. And all the other children he hoped they would have one day.

He wanted to wrap his perfect family in cotton wool and keep them locked away for ever from the outside world, so no one and nothing would ever have the power to hurt them. He wanted to protect them with his money, his resources and the last breath in his body. He wanted to cocoon them for ever in the love that still took his breath away every time he laid eyes on either one of them.

But that was the coward's way out.

Because he'd seen the look of excitement in Megan's eyes, seen how enthusiastic she was about this new opportunity. And he knew if he loved her, he could not kill that joy—however great his need to protect her from harm.

Damn it. But loving someone more than life itself— the way he loved Megan and Issy—was fraught with so many complications. Complications and difficult choices that he often found it extremely hard to even comprehend, let alone solve.

But then the words Megan had said to him a year ago, in the courthouse in Manhattan, echoed in his head. The words he had had to repeat to himself so many times since: when Megan had been curled over the toilet bowl and throwing up each morning through most of the months of her pregnancy; when he had endured the terror of watching her bring their child into the world through twelve gut-wrenching hours of labour; when he'd held the tiny, vulnerable and unbearably precious life they'd made together in his hands for the first time. The words he knew he would be repeating to himself for the rest of his life: when Issy took her first step; when he had to leave her on her first day of school; when he taught her how to ride a bike, drive a car, sail a boat, fly a helicopter; when she went off to Harvard or Yale—because, obviously, his daughter was going to be the smartest, bravest, most brilliant child the world had ever seen.

To have the joy you have to overcome your fear.

He kissed his fingertips and pressed them to the soft skin of his daughter's forehead; her tiny chest rose and fell in the regular rhythm of deep sleep. Relief eased some of the tightness in his chest. Thank goodness, he wouldn't have to face most of those fears with his daughter for a little while at least.

Walking back into the bedroom, he spotted Megan sitting up in their big bed, her arms wrapped around her drawn-up knees.

'Dario? I need to know what you think,' she said, her anxiety tempered with determination. 'About me taking the job?'

He climbed onto the bed, then gathered her into his arms. He held her tight, let the swell of arousal—that was always there when she was near him—help him to push out the words.

'You want to take this job?' he asked as he kissed her hair, even though he already knew the answer.

'Yes, I do.' She swung round in his arms, the eagerness on her face crucifying him a little more. 'I thought it all through about Issy's care while I'm at work. Lydia is fabulous with her, and she's happy to step in. And we've got more than enough other staff to take up the slack.'

He'd employed Lydia Brady as soon as he and Megan had moved into the new town house he'd bought on the Upper East Side—concerned that the penthouse apartment might not be suitable for a child. He'd also insisted on hiring three additional staff. Something he knew Megan still struggled with. He was forever coming home and finding the staff helping Megan with some charity project or other that had nothing to do with their domestic duties.

'And anyway, I'm only going to be working three hours a day to start,' his wife continued. 'I told them I want to take the time to wean Issy properly.'

'Shh, Megan.' He tucked her hair behind her ears, allowed his thumbs to skim down her cheeks. 'You don't have to say any more.'

Dio, *but I love this woman so much.*

'If you want to do this thing,' he added, 'I would never stand in your way.'

'Really?' She smiled. 'Because I thought... When you walked out with Issy like that, I thought you were upset about the idea. That you were going to object to it.'

He shook his head. He wasn't the only one with insecurities. Why did he find that so comforting all of a sudden?

'I could never refuse something so important to you,' he said, but then he smiled, enjoying the role of devil's advocate. 'But if I did, what would you do?'

The quick, seductive smile captivated him as she reached up to cradle his cheeks. 'Then I guess I would have to convince you,' she whispered against his lips.

She set her mouth on his. The heat surged at the seductive licks of her tongue.

He chuckled, the sound deep and so full of contentment. A contentment he'd never believed could be his. Her delighted answering smile made his heart thunder in his chest.

They would be okay. This job would be okay. He had to let her have her freedom despite his fears. And Megan need never know that he would hire one of Jared's security team to watch over her while she was in Brooklyn.

And if she did find out, they could always negotiate. Because if there was one thing his wife was an expert at, it was negotiation.

Scooping her up, he sat her in his lap, held her firmly when she wriggled, inflaming his desires still more.

'So you think you can convince me?' He cupped her breast, licking at the rigid tip through the sheer fabric of her nightgown. Arousal surged into his groin when she arched into his mouth, responding with enthusiasm to the erotic torture as always. 'Perhaps I will convince you first?' he teased.

She grasped his head and pulled his mouth up to hers. The kiss was long and deep before she drew back.

'You're on, big boy,' she said, clearly relishing the erotic challenge—even though she had to know she'd already won.

His loyalty, his trust and every single piece of his heart.

* * * * *

If you enjoyed
THE VIRGIN'S SHOCK BABY
why not explore these other
ONE NIGHT WITH CONSEQUENCES *stories?*

THE BOSS'S NINE-MONTH NEGOTIATION
by Maya Blake
THE PREGNANT KAVAKOS BRIDE
by Sharon Kendrick
A RING FOR THE GREEK'S BABY
by Melanie Milburne
ENGAGED FOR HER ENEMY'S HEIR
by Kate Hewitt

Available now!

MILLS & BOON®
Hardback – October 2017

ROMANCE

Claimed for the Leonelli Legacy	Lynne Graham
The Italian's Pregnant Prisoner	Maisey Yates
Buying His Bride of Convenience	Michelle Smart
The Tycoon's Marriage Deal	Melanie Milburne
Undone by the Billionaire Duke	Caitlin Crews
His Majesty's Temporary Bride	Annie West
Bound by the Millionaire's Ring	Dani Collins
The Virgin's Shock Baby	Heidi Rice
Whisked Away by Her Sicilian Boss	Rebecca Winters
The Sheikh's Pregnant Bride	Jessica Gilmore
A Proposal from the Italian Count	Lucy Gordon
Claiming His Secret Royal Heir	Nina Milne
Sleigh Ride with the Single Dad	Alison Roberts
A Firefighter in Her Stocking	Janice Lynn
A Christmas Miracle	Amy Andrews
Reunited with Her Surgeon Prince	Marion Lennox
Falling for Her Fake Fiancé	Sue MacKay
The Family She's Longed For	Lucy Clark
Billionaire Boss, Holiday Baby	Janice Maynard
Billionaire's Baby Bind	Katherine Garbera

MILLS & BOON®
Large Print – October 2017

ROMANCE

Sold for the Greek's Heir	Lynne Graham
The Prince's Captive Virgin	Maisey Yates
The Secret Sanchez Heir	Cathy Williams
The Prince's Nine-Month Scandal	Caitlin Crews
Her Sinful Secret	Jane Porter
The Drakon Baby Bargain	Tara Pammi
Xenakis's Convenient Bride	Dani Collins
Her Pregnancy Bombshell	Liz Fielding
Married for His Secret Heir	Jennifer Faye
Behind the Billionaire's Guarded Heart	Leah Ashton
A Marriage Worth Saving	Therese Beharrie

HISTORICAL

The Debutante's Daring Proposal	Annie Burrows
The Convenient Felstone Marriage	Jenni Fletcher
An Unexpected Countess	Laurie Benson
Claiming His Highland Bride	Terri Brisbin
Marrying the Rebellious Miss	Bronwyn Scott

MEDICAL

Their One Night Baby	Carol Marinelli
Forbidden to the Playboy Surgeon	Fiona Lowe
A Mother to Make a Family	Emily Forbes
The Nurse's Baby Secret	Janice Lynn
The Boss Who Stole Her Heart	Jennifer Taylor
Reunited by Their Pregnancy Surprise	Louisa Heaton

MILLS & BOON®
Hardback – November 2017

ROMANCE

The Italian's Christmas Secret	Sharon Kendrick
A Diamond for the Sheikh's Mistress	Abby Green
The Sultan Demands His Heir	Maya Blake
Claiming His Scandalous Love-Child	Julia James
Valdez's Bartered Bride	Rachael Thomas
The Greek's Forbidden Princess	Annie West
Kidnapped for the Tycoon's Baby	Louise Fuller
A Night, A Consequence, A Vow	Angela Bissell
Christmas with Her Millionaire Boss	Barbara Wallace
Snowbound with an Heiress	Jennifer Faye
Newborn Under the Christmas Tree	Sophie Pembroke
His Mistletoe Proposal	Christy McKellen
The Spanish Duke's Holiday Proposal	Robin Gianna
The Rescue Doc's Christmas Miracle	Amalie Berlin
Christmas with Her Daredevil Doc	Kate Hardy
Their Pregnancy Gift	Kate Hardy
A Family Made at Christmas	Scarlet Wilson
Their Mistletoe Baby	Karin Baine
The Texan Takes a Wife	Charlene Sands
Twins for the Billionaire	Sarah M. Anderson

MILLS & BOON®
Large Print – November 2017

ROMANCE

The Pregnant Kavakos Bride	Sharon Kendrick
The Billionaire's Secret Princess	Caitlin Crews
Sicilian's Baby of Shame	Carol Marinelli
The Secret Kept from the Greek	Susan Stephens
A Ring to Secure His Crown	Kim Lawrence
Wedding Night with Her Enemy	Melanie Milburne
Salazar's One-Night Heir	Jennifer Hayward
The Mysterious Italian Houseguest	Scarlet Wilson
Bound to Her Greek Billionaire	Rebecca Winters
Their Baby Surprise	Katrina Cudmore
The Marriage of Inconvenience	Nina Singh

HISTORICAL

Ruined by the Reckless Viscount	Sophia James
Cinderella and the Duke	Janice Preston
A Warriner to Rescue Her	Virginia Heath
Forbidden Night with the Warrior	Michelle Willingham
The Foundling Bride	Helen Dickson

MEDICAL

Mummy, Nurse...Duchess?	Kate Hardy
Falling for the Foster Mum	Karin Baine
The Doctor and the Princess	Scarlet Wilson
Miracle for the Neurosurgeon	Lynne Marshall
English Rose for the Sicilian Doc	Annie Claydon
Engaged to the Doctor Sheikh	Meredith Webber

MILLS & BOON®

Why shop at millsandboon.co.uk?

Each year, thousands of romance readers find their perfect read at millsandboon.co.uk. That's because we're passionate about bringing you the very best romantic fiction. Here are some of the advantages of shopping at www.millsandboon.co.uk:

* **Get new books first**—you'll be able to buy your favourite books one month before they hit the shops

* **Get exclusive discounts**—you'll also be able to buy our specially created monthly collections, with up to 50% off the RRP

* **Find your favourite authors**—latest news, interviews and new releases for all your favourite authors and series on our website, plus ideas for what to try next

* **Join in**—once you've bought your favourite books, don't forget to register with us to rate, review and join in the discussions

Visit **www.millsandboon.co.uk**
for all this and more today!

AP